Entry into Jerusalem

Entry into Jerusalem

STANLEY MIDDLETON

NEW AMSTERDAM
New York

First published in the United States of America in 1988 by
NEW AMSTERDAM BOOKS
171 Madison Avenue
New York, N.Y. 10016

Published by arrangement with
Century Hutchinson Ltd., London.

Library of Congress Cataloging-in-Publication Data

Middleton, Stanley, 1919-
Entry into Jerusalem/Stanley Middleton.

I. Title.
PR6063.I25E5   1988   88-31300
ISBN 0-941533-46-8

Printed in the United States of America.

This book is printed on acid-free paper.

1

Black trees rose to the left, wintry branches laced intricately against the sky. Below them long, bleached grass shook, the clumps alive in a leap of the wind. On the right, clouds were breaking, and wide bars of sunlight fell obliquely to the earth, the edges of each beam straight-ruled in parallel, misting in gold the distant city spires, the tower-blocks, the factories. Above the clouds, the sky stretched striking blue, over the silver contours, but again a darkening shower blotted the extreme, fading end of the horizon.

John Worth shook his head, nibbled the end of his brush. The doorbell had rung.

Without hurry he replaced the implement, shuffled along the passage, caught up still in the slow desperation of his painting.

'Oh, you're in, then. Couldn't see a light. Thought you might be out gallivanting somewhere.' Hoarse, hearty voice.

Worth did not answer, or move.

'Are you busy? Shall I call another time?'

'Come in.' He stood aside.

'Are you sure? I don't want to interrupt anything.' The visitor, broad-shouldered in mackintosh and cloth cap, did not alter his position on the threshold until a second invitation had been issued. 'Are you painting? I'm not going to stop you in that case. I'm not here for any real purpose.'

They processed in single file to the studio, built on to the back of the kitchen, half an old wash-house, half an addition in new emplastered brick, with a wide window facing north, masked now with brown velvet curtains.

'Aren't you cold in here?' the visitor blustered. Worth pointed without conviction towards an electric fire and began to clear away his materials, not unsociably but without speaking, before washing his hands at the sink.

The other man, Thomas Theodore Turnbull, stood with legs apart in front of the painting, clasping his hands behind his back, then swinging them outwards to slap the pockets of his mackintosh.

'That's new,' he said. 'Where is it?'

'Burwell Park. And my head.' Worth watched him, turning his eyes from face to picture and back.

'Are you pleased with it?'

'Never thought. I've worked on it for a day or two. It's as good as finished. I'll tell you next week if it's any use.'

'Why can't you tell me now?'

'I'm still dabbing at it. Altering. Poking it around. Now I shall stop. If I want to continue by next Friday, I haven't done it properly.'

'You'll play about again?'

'No. I don't like large afterthoughts with watercolours. Too tricky by half. I'll just have a completely new shot and hope it improves.' All the time he talked John Worth methodically cleaned and cleared up, closing lids, wiping surfaces. 'This is my third tidy-away tonight. One just half an hour ago, two since you've been in here. I always leave something about. Or I'm a head-case. I'm worse at squaring up than at painting, and that's not saying much.' He washed his hands again unenthusiastically.

'It's the pattern,' Turnbull said, still in front of the picture.

'You don't have to comment, you know.'

'When I come in here, it's my pleasure to say my piece. And your,' he wagged his thick first finger at it, 'bit of a thing here is, partakes of the nature of, an abstract.' He grinned at his words, mockingly, but he cocked his head to one side, looking again at the picture, not at the painter. 'Is that right?'

'Possibly.' Worth draped his towel on a small clothes-horse, and rubbed his large, thin hands up and down the chest of an unclean khaki pullover.

'Words don't mean much. Or do they?' Turnbull sighed deeply as if he had questioned himself beyond all comprehension but had failed the test. At the same time his face remained a cheerful red, and his yellow-white hair in a parted, schoolboy neatness.

Worth switched off the bar fire, waited at the door. The two men cluttered the kitchen until Turnbull took himself off to stand with his back to the central-heating boiler.

'Beer or coffee?'

'What do you usually have?'

'Coffee,' Worth said, 'but I don't often have you as a visitor.'

'We'll have that, then. As if nothing had happened.'

'Has it?'

'Has what?'

'Nothing happened.'

Tap water sang into the kettle. The host mooched about the kitchen, placing china, opening a packet of biscuits, finding a milk bottle. Though Turnbull did not shift his position, standing with his legs sturdily apart, he gave the appearance of powerful movement in that he rolled his head, still capped, and his shoulders, a tethered bison.

'Take your hat and coat off.' Worth carried them to the pegs in the hall. Without his coat, in ginger, creased tweeds Turnbull looked broader than ever. 'How are things in Grange Avenue?'

'Thriving, if the noise is anything to go by.'

'Where's Millicent?'

'At her pottery class. Denman Street. Run by a fellow called Wilkinson. Is he any good?'

'I don't know him.'

'You don't live on this earth, do you?' At this apparently satisfactory gibe, Turnbull delicately extracted a stool and parked himself, where he stroked his thighs, straddling. Nearly fifty, a schoolmaster, he'd become scandalously entangled with a girl younger than his daughter and his son, and had married her ten months ago. His school, it was rumoured, had tried to transfer him, or sack him, but he'd resisted blandishments and threats, and had stayed where he wanted to be, nobody's enemy but the headmaster's, the governors' and his own. Seven years ago he and Worth had been colleagues for four terms, never particularly intimate, but the older man had once or twice conveyed to the younger a sense of admiration, grudging perhaps, expressed critically, but strong. This Worth couldn't

7

teach, and never would be able to, except perhaps to one or two gifted souls who did not need instruction, who would find their own way whatever happened, but he was in Ted Turnbull's book a prodigy, a talent among mediocrities.

'I don't know what we shall do with young Worth,' the headmaster had complained. 'His classes are all over him.'

'You be careful what he does with you,' Turnbull answered. The headmaster corrugated his high, bald brow; at the time he liked his deputy, depended on him, expected him to talk sense.

The pair settled to their coffee, Turnbull dunking his biscuits, squatting as if, every minute, he'd overbalance.

'Did you do sketches on the ground?' he asked. 'Out in the park?'

'Yes. I was there again this morning.'

'The sky wasn't anything like that.'

'No. There's always something else to look at.'

'You use a camera sometimes?'

'Yes. I'd sooner sketch. But I've had some first-rate ideas from photographs. Nothing against them.'

'Your picture worries me.' Turnbull's voice slowed to a drawl, spluttered through a mesh of biscuit. John Worth watched, eyes alight, mouth crooked in mischief.

'Oh, oh,' he enunciated, acting.

'It has creation about it. As if you made the world again. Used the materials, but rearranged them. Sometimes the result's not so good, quite, er, as the original.'

'And never as complex.'

'That's right. But when I see some of your pictures, I get a twist in the bowels, because you've done something not many others could. God's too fancy, too varied, too explosive; but you fine Him down. I'm not the only one to say so. You make him graspable.'

'Have more coffee.'

'I will. You can afford it, the prices you charge for your daubs these days. Didn't think there was that sort of money about.'

'You'd be surprised. Styles Warner aren't doing too well, but Miriam and Victor will keep me solvent. And Burden Brothers.' He pulled a letter from his kitchen drawer. 'Look at

8

this.' Turnbull sipped noisily, perused the headed sheet once, then twice, poked it back into its envelope.

'I say, I say.' It was a preliminary inquiry about a commission for a mural in a house in London. 'Will you do it?'

'I'll go up and look. I can charge them for that. The client's an Arab.'

'How do you know?'

'They phoned as well.'

'Must be keen. Must be. Patronage of oil sheiks. Will Styles Warner let you go?'

'I only turn in two days a week for them now.'

'Have you made sketches?'

'You keep asking me that. No. Not till I've seen the room, or photographs of it. And until I've heard their views.'

'Belly dancers. Houris. The zenana. Though very likely the silly bastards want oaks and elms and hawthorn hedges with wild crows flying.'

'That's why they've chosen me?'

'Probably.'

'The harmless Englishman?'

Turnbull sucked his thumb, like a big baby, and made no demur, paid no attention, as Worth again blackly filled his friend's mug, before trickling another inch into his own small china cup.

'They're playing up at home,' the visitor announced, glowering at the gilt knob of a kitchen cupboard.

'Natalie?'

'No. Piers and Millicent.'

'Hasn't he gone back to the university yet?' Piers, in his third year towards a D.Phil. at Oxford, was two years older than his stepmother.

'No. He's wasting his time there, he says. Not that I believe him. He knows it annoys me. I think he works hard, if only because it's in his own interest. But he niggles at her. Isn't she bored washing pots and baking pies?'

'And is she?'

'She tries to argue with him, and that's just what he wants. He sits there with his legs stuck out and his gut full of her

9

cooking explaining that she was meant for something more than domestic slavery.'

'And she loses her temper?'

'Not really. She's flustered, in a way. And worse so when I intervene to tell him to get off his fat arse to give her a hand. But no. She blushes, and runs away, and thinks of something else to say in the kitchen, equally ill-directed. I'm not criticizing her. Her virtues are many, but maintaining public argument is not one of them. What are you grinning at?'

'You sound like the Latin exercises we used to do. "Though she was a woman of many talents, eloquence was not numbered amongst them." '

'Those sentences stuffed with the subjunctive very often state in a formal and old-fashioned style something about the way we live and move and have our being, and which we're gradually losing the art of expressing, with our grunts and farts and telly and jargon.'

'Well, now.'

'We're an illiterate society. Still it doesn't sort out my domestic upsets, does it? I can't help feeling that Milly wants him to snap at her, and goad her; she thinks it's all part of the education she abandoned, that somehow she's improving her mind.'

'Is she?'

'Not really. And it riles me, I can tell you.' Turnbull tweaked a curl at the crown of his head. 'And then that frightens her. She looks like the pale waif who sat at the front of my WEA class three years ago. Eyes like saucers, listening to the word of the prophet. I thought I was getting her out of that.'

'How?' Worth, innocently.

'Not with local history. In bed.'

'Oh.'

' "Oh" be buggered.' Turnbull rubbed his hands together, ploughman's palms, and grinned. 'But it lifts me to come here and complain, and have a look at a new picture, and know that something's going on in the world that's beyond me. In a minute or two I'll be out there singing in the street.'

'What will you sing?'

10

' "Show me the way to go home." ' Both men laughed.

Worth took a pair of glasses from his pocket, donned them. Like him they were pale, delicately made, large, not quite in true, rather dusty. Turnbull snatched a loose pair from the top pocket of his jacket, rammed them on his nose; these were black, thick-rimmed, with earpieces nearly half an inch wide. At once he seemed more fearsome, fiercer.

'There we are, then,' he said. 'We've had a good look at each other. When are you off to London?' He poked the spectacles away.

'Tomorrow.'

'You don't waste much time.' Turnbull jangled the money in his trouser pocket. 'Can I bring Milly up some time to have a look at you?'

'With pleasure.'

'I should want you to talk to her, explain what you're doing. She's an enthusiast for words. That's why she tangles with Piers.'

'I'm not sure that what I do is susceptible to rational explanation.'

'No wonder you didn't succeed as a schoolmaster. I'm explaining, words in torrent if not spate, what I don't understand all day. But you do as you like. Is this potter she goes to a good talker? Oh, you don't know him.'

Worth did not answer, appeared mildly entranced as he sat with chin in hands.

'What's the programme for the rest of the evening?' Turnbull asked, not confidently.

'I might read. Or just sit. Or put a record on.'

'Do you have music on when you're painting? She told me to ask you that.'

'Sometimes.'

'Anything in particular?'

'Sibelius. Starts me off. But I don't hear it once I've begun.'

'You don't hear it. Is it very soft?'

'No. Not really. But as far as I know I don't hear it. Subconsciously I might. I can't say. I'm trying to remember, but sometimes I find the turntable spinning when the automatic

11

cut-off has failed. And the poof-poof as it goes round disturbs me.'

'She'll ask you what painters she should admire.'

'See.'

'Eh?'

'See, not admire. I'd send her to look at things.'

'That you admire. Boils down to much the same.'

'I'm not sure.' Worth shook his head. 'Not sure at all.'

Turnbull knitted his brows into burly dunes, blowing his lips out and finally rising to return his stool to its place.

'Many thanks for the coffee. She'll expect me to let myself in dead on a quarter to nine. Don't get lost tomorrow.'

'No fear.'

'I don't think you would, either.'

Turnbull allowed his friend to show him to coat, then door, where he remarked on the starlight and bundled his hands into gauntlets. He closed the wrought-iron garden gate without a clang.

2

February sunshine warmed the streets of London.

John Worth stood outside the Burden Gallery, uncomfortable and excited, waiting to be driven to St John's Wood. His driver–escort, George Walden, a frail, elderly man who stood not much above five feet tall, confidently cocked the round head, topped with fine grey hair, too large for the small frame. He spoke with a foreign accent almost overlaid with aristocratic English pronunciation that enhanced its alien nature, pushed it near uniqueness. His small, manicured, beautifully shaped right hand constantly stroked, or caressed, from brow to crown, the fine hair which both covered and revealed the pinkness of his scalp. He dressed with care; the tiny shoes were round-toed.

'I have the keys,' he said. 'We will talk there.'

He had been introduced to Worth as a director of the gallery in a businesslike ten minutes spent with Victor Burden, who had offered coffee and made encouraging noises about another exhibition.

'We can sell your work,' Victor had said. 'Not profitably enough yet, but. As soon as this commission dropped on my desk, I suggested you. Albert agreed.' The elder brother, the financial king. 'So I want you to run along with George here. Listen to what he tells you. He's shrewd. He's an expert. He has influence. He also does not want to paint pictures. Discuss it. With him.' He'd shaken his head, lugubriously, then Worth's hand, and had drifted out from the office leaving his coffee untouched.

Now, in a large Volvo, Worth enjoyed the sunshine. Walden's small legs had no difficulty with the pedals so that he drove abstractedly as if he'd more to occupy himself with than the bright whirl of traffic. The few remarks he made concerned other drivers, one-way streets, a pedestrian, road repairs. Just before they parked he pointed out Lord's cricket ground, said he had spent some afternoons there the previous summer.

'Did you ever play?' Worth asked.

'My God.' Walden laughed, as if at a joke, but patted an ornate Victorian pillar box with his miniature hand as they walked the last yards.

Worth offered a guarded word of admiration about the large houses.

'Yes, pop stars only can afford them,' Walden answered and that gave him satisfaction so that he sharply pulled at his expensive gloves and hummed Bartók, Kodály. 'There might be workmen about, one never knows.' Certainly a pile of planed planks and spars lay under weighted plastic outside the door, which was locked. Walden, fiddling with his keys, flared his nostrils, breathed deeply as if testing the quality of the air. 'We shall step inside so that you will immediately see what is to be your province.' He quietly opened the heavy door, pointed briefly, then stroked a lion's head brass knocker, then shut Worth and himself inside a small foyer, rather dark, with three

13

stained-glass windows and thick bristle doormats covering the floor. Another key was produced, an equally weighty door negotiated, and they were in the hall.

The room was large, square; four, black-brown pillars in mottled marble rose in the centre. Windows on the left lit the place so that it seemed lighter than the foyer, clean, clinically prepared with the walls cream-oatmeal, and the cornices white. Walden threw out a flattened hand like a tiny traffic policeman.

'There.'

He indicated a section of the wall, five yards by six feet, framed with elegant plaster.

'Just that?' Worth asked.

'You've other ideas?'

'There'll be plenty of space. Outside the mural.'

'Is that a disadvantage?'

'I'm thinking aloud,' Worth grumbled.

'Exactly, exactly.' Walden led his man to the wall, which he tapped with a fingernail. 'The plaster is smooth.'

'Lights?' Worth asked.

The other crossed to a battery of brass-headed switches, lit chandeliers with sudden brilliance, and smiled as if the whole operation had been directed towards this one climax of brightness. He waited for Worth who stood there, peering about, his overcoat shabby in the steady effulgence.

'How shall we fill it?' Walden asked, finally impatient.

'Switch the lights off. Must cost a fortune.' He was instantly obeyed.

'Have you an idea?' Walden, returning, alert, tip-toe.

'One.'

'Can you talk about it?'

He signalled Worth to a row of chairs, polished like brown glass, though sawdust, curls of shavings, small offcuts littered the floor. Walden seated himself, hands extended, ready to be amazed. Still Worth shuffled around.

'Will they carpet the floor?'

'I should think not.' Oaken, beautifully kept parquet, every snug edge demonstrating craftsmanship. 'I would not myself.' Walden attended, one-handed, delicately, to his hair

14

once more. 'Does it make a difference?' Now he sounded exotically foreign as though he matched his accent to the outlandish nature of the question. Worth completed his tour, walking straight past the chair Walden occupied in expectation, ended up for the second time by the windows.

Neither spoke for a time. The radiator under Worth's hands struck cold.

'The other night . . .' he began.

'Ah,' Walden, rewarded, restored to a belief in rationality.

'The other night I was standing in my front room and saw some motorist, headlamps full on, drive straight into my drive to turn round. The gates were fastened back. Came right up and in. And then he stalled his engine. Now there's a rose bush in front of the side window of the bay; big, strong-growing thing; I let it rip. Canary Bird. Covered with little yellow flowers. Early. Too soon for a rose, some say. Not now, of course. Great spikes on it. When I do prune it, it lets you know. The light through this was flung up onto the white ceiling, a widening mesh of shadows. I'd never thought of it, you know.'

'Why should you?'

'Because I'm supposed to be an artist. That's why.' He spat air past his lips with exasperation. 'Went straight out and made two, three sketches on a pencil block. Not good enough. Tried again next morning. I even stuck my van in the drive with the headlights on. Not so powerful as I remembered it, and that's a good sign.'

'I see.'

'That's what I want to do there.' Worth pointed to the bare plaster, and Walden rose to advance towards it. Suddenly Worth's eyes dropped as he pushed his hands into his trouser pockets to rattle his change. 'What do you think?'

'No,' said Walden, cooing. 'No.'

'What d'you mean? No?'

'You asked me a question. You have my answer. I do not see it. You could convince me by sketches, but it sounds mere pattern, complicated design, in black and white. The client wants colour. Rich colours. Dark reds, smooth green, purple, solid blue, like a stained-glass window.' Walden raised his

15

minute palm, pushed the air towards Worth, for silence. 'He admired your illustrations to *King Arthur*.'

'That was a children's book.'

'My friend, my friend.'

Worth grinned, baring his teeth.

'The client is a cultivated Arab, connected with royalty, I'm told, and has received his education in the West, in Paris as well as London. He wants something that will stand off the wall in the green light of day as well as by electricity. I can't say I blame him. I think as he does. You will, I expect, do as you like, but I ask you, not advise, certainly not order you, to try out my idea. I tell you why. You will do your pictures of rose-shadows whatever happens with us. Try this other thing.' They both stared at the wall. 'I have photographs of the place, measurements,' he tapped his briefcase, 'now that you have seen the site. We will look round the house, stand here again, and then you will return home and provide sketches.'

He marched out, up the wide, newly painted uncarpeted staircase, not waiting for his companion, not looking back.

Some of the rooms were furnished ready for occupation, while others were stripped to the floorboards, wood-dusty, with a sawing-horse, a gaping bag of tools, a blowlamp. Whether a place was chaotic or in order, Walden took up a position, drew Worth's attention to proportions or fireplaces, to window size, and once he beckoned his companion to his side so that he could point out a mere area of dark roof and patch of white wall, a Georgian house he admired. He lectured, unemphatically, running his small hand backwards above his scalp, his voice crackling as if he'd been bawling odds all day at the street corner. When the tour had concluded, he hurried back into the hall, ahead of Worth, to stand facing the empty tablet.

'That is the house,' he said. 'This is your space.'

The small, elegant figure annoyed Worth; the cut of the overcoat, the excellence of gold links in much-exposed cuffs, the grey trousers, sparrow's legs, but most of all the confident cock of the head, superiority of stance.

'Well, Mr Worth. Look your fill.'

'I've looked.'

16

'Does anything strike you?'

'No. Should it?'

'No. I am giving you the opportunity to comment. Some chance remark may prove invaluable, help settle your course.'

'I'm a painter. That's not got much to do with talking.'

Walden tapped the side of his nose, inducing a trance or a sneeze. He then nodded heavily, as if his doll's head would roll off, rearranged his undisturbed hair and said that though it was early they would take lunch.

'When we have finished we can return here, if you so wish.'

'Stop wittling,' Worth said. Dialect provided the only answer to cosmopolitan ease.

'As you please.'

They rode again in the Volvo, lunched at a fish restaurant where Walden ordered oysters for himself; the white wine was dry, biting the tongue. Worth wolfed his trout, turned down a further offered visit to the plaster, was presented with a folio of photographs, was dropped, as he asked, at the nearest tube station.

'Goodbye, Mr Worth. I look forward to your sketches.'

Worth thanked him, wry-necked, for his hospitality and stood to watch the grey car glide away. Head slightly muzzy with two glasses of wine, he wondered where Walden's next call would take him. Perhaps his departure had ended the day's work, but it seemed unlikely; the imp would dictate letters, to be typed electrically out, thick watermarked paper, the address heavily, blackly embossed, and sign them with a neat illegible scratch. What was his provenance? Neither homosexual nor provincial, the man seemed divorced from such human considerations as race or passion or family. Yet he watched cricket in the summer.

For a minute the painter eyed from his pavement three men excavating earth round a clutch of cables; finally successful, they did not speak, but stared silently as if they had discovered the utterly unexpected. Worth stared with them, but they paid no heed to the figure above while they dabbled down, unseriously, with a spade, as if waiting for, anticipating some further revelation. One clambered out and lit a fag; his

17

companions continued their dumb vigil. The man with the cigarette nodded a cheerful greeting at him and Worth, caught out, legged it for the station.

On the north bound train he sat slackly observing the death of daylight. When he emerged the sky was quite dark, but he decided against a taxi, having no time to save, and walked through the streets to the bus terminus. The rush hour was over, but windows shone fiercely and the subways were not short of hurrying people. He would draw, he thought, three Rastafarians on a seat in an enclosed shopping precinct, by a fountain, backed by leggy plants, and reflected in the black row of glass doors. Outside again, he noted the spire of a church, dark against darkness, while below, the art déco shop fronts were hung lazily with light. No colour, no richness, only yellow against black; nothing of medieval, nothing to fill the houses of millionaires.

At home the two bills which had arrived by the morning's post were where he had thrown them on his kitchen table. He decided against cooking the chops in the fridge, and calming himself with weak tea and the *Guardian*, he fell uncomfortably asleep in his armchair. He woke puzzled and angry, but filed Walden's wallet of instructions without opening it. Now he pulled down the portfolio of sketches for *King Arthur*; prancing steeds, greaves, the helmet and the helmet-feather, red-roofed houses, distant hillocks, slender leaning silver birches in the foreground, or moonlight on the mere and the castles rising from the streaks of starlit mist. Pastiche, nothing of himself; a hurried job for a friend, which he'd enjoyed. A huge, muted-gold harvest moon over a wood splitting with menace, and the silhouette of a knight, poised, posed, artificial. Worth grimaced, admiring his skill, but told himself, unconvincingly, that this had nothing to do with John Worth, was conjuring, art-school foolery. He straightened the drawings, packed them away, closed the sliding doors of his cupboards and went out into the studio.

The cold struck into his shoulders; he could not stay there. If only he smoked he could then occupy the next minutes without disorganization. Certainly he would not draw tonight, but he

18

wished to spin ideas in his head. That he did not do well; he thought, felt more forcibly with a pencil or brush in his hand, but he'd show his disdain for Walden by sitting in an armchair and filling that lozenge of plaster with the raggle-taggle of his mind. Motorway lights; chrysanthemums big as bronze foot-balls; cloth-capped men with scarves sliding on a frozen pond; terraced slate-topped houses, chimneys palled with smoke, snaking uphill in untidy parallel. The seaside, but with no thyme-fragrant, heather-tipped cliffs, only bony legs in scuffed and littered sand, stripes of deckchairs heavy with flesh and sweat.

He began to excite himself, reached for a pencil, checked the movement; Walden would get nothing tonight.

3

Ursula Quinn phoned, interrupting his idle session, invited him round to her house to report on his London visit. At 8.30 he had no wish to venture out, but could not immediately demur and, replacing tie and shoes, glanced from under a lifted curtain at the weather. The moon spread lurid blue light in his garden as he let himself out by the back gate, in the uncomfortably sharp air, onto a sparkling path. Ten minutes brought him to Victoria Street.

'You said you'd ring.' Ursula remonstrated with him as soon as she had closed the door.

'You didn't give me a chance.'

'Would you have rung, then?'

'Probably not.'

She kept him in the passage for preliminary questions about his trip so that he knew her father was at home. A tall girl with bushy dark hair, blue eyes, Ursula held herself upright, pushing one hand now behind her against the wallpaper, as she spoke to him in a whisper. He offered her a few sentences as he removed his coat, so that they shared a half-dozen facts before she led him to the living room.

Her father sat at his ease in front of the fire. In his chair he appeared small, with a pinched face, thin lips, narrow trunk, though Worth knew he stood nearly six feet. His slippers were razored to accommodate bunions; his right arm circled, weirdly high, an unlighted cigarette perched between fingers.

'Home is the sailor,' he said, 'home from the sea.'

His voice matched the peaky, bloodless face; it attempted to rouse no interest and Worth had no reply.

'Sit down, man. Urse'll bring us a cup of tea.'

'There's no need.'

'You speak for yourself.'

The daughter drew up a chair by the table and her father grimaced maliciously at her.

'You've been hobnobbing, they tell me,' Quinn began again.

'I'm "they",' Ursula said.

'A plural of politeness.' Worth spoke and watched Quinn pick up the newspaper, roughly tented at his feet, select a page, an edge, tear off a strip to fold a spill. The cigarette now wobbled in his mouth. With a hutching forward of the chair Quinn leaned down to light the fag, knock out the flame, drop the charred paper in the hearth.

'Waste not, want not,' he answered his daughter's accusatory stare. 'I can use that again. Newspapers are made from trees.' The girl rose, threw the remains into the fire. Her father, leaning back, exhaled ragged smoke, coughed with the luxury. 'And how were the bright lights?'

Worth repeated what he had told the daughter.

'So you haven't actually got the commission yet?' the man wheezed.

'No.'

'You might have wasted a day going up there?'

'Yes. Except I shall claim for expenses and sketches.'

'John doesn't waste time. He's seen something today.' Priggish.

'What's that, then?' Yapped like a terrier.

'I don't know, do I? How could I? Ask him if you must know.'

20

'Speaking out of ignorance again?' Quinn loosed a phlegmy volley of coughing. 'Why don't you let the man talk for himself. He doesn't want women explaining what he means, any more than I do.'

'I rather like it,' Worth said.

Quinn did not spit, but appeared ready to do so.

'Get us a cup of tea, Urse,' he begged. 'My throat's like a lime kiln.'

'Stop smoking, then.' But she made for the kitchen.

'She's got the temperament you ought to have,' Quinn said. 'She's the artist without the talent. You let 'em stand there and piss all over you. Not her.'

'Oh, yes.'

'These London flash-bags. Stand up; sit down. To the front, salute. And you do it.'

'Is that bad?'

'Either you've got something to offer, something they want, or you haven't. They wouldn't push her about. You're somebody.'

'What makes you so sure?'

'You wouldn't have these exhibitions if they didn't think there was something there.'

'My dear man . . .' Worth said listlessly.

'My dear man,' Quinn mocked. 'You'd better marry her, or get her to work as your agent. Don't you like women? Sexually?'

That the advice, the blunt questions went unanswered seemed not to worry Ursula's father, who fumbled furtively for a dirty handkerchief, blew his nose needlessly loud and sighed, shifting on bony hams. He pored deep into the fire, as if he had given the visitor up, while Worth looking round the room counted the number of ways in which it was uncomfortable. Nothing matched; pictures hung crooked; chair seats struck hard; the fire scorched close shins but did nothing to temper draughts from the two doors.

'Something'll happen to that girl before so long,' Quinn said, nasally.

'Such as?'

'She'll up and leave home. Oh, I know that's what you're pressing her to do all the time. She knows which side her bread's buttered, but she'll be off before so long.'

'Would it worry you?'

'Who's to say? Depends, don't it? I wouldn't want her sharing bed and board with you, for one.' Quinn thumbnailed the line of almost invisible moustache which bordered his upper lip. 'She'll be no better off with you than with me.'

Ursula returned.

'We're settling your future,' Worth said.

'Don't bother.'

The voice reminded him of her father's; whenever the two were together she seemed to imitate Quinn's malicious lethargy.

After the girl had poured the tea, Worth offered them a description of the London house, of the wall he was to cover.

'What do you think?' Ursula asked, keenly.

'I'm not sure.'

'Do you want the job?'

'Not really. But then again, I do. I have to force myself to look carefully at new-fangled notions. I want to stay here, but another side of me is rushing up there already.'

'You'll be disappointed if it falls through?'

'Yes. I shall.'

'You make him do it, Urse,' Quinn ordered.

'How can I?'

'Has she any influence on you, then?'

Worth did not answer, wishing he could disentangle himself from family bickering. He would sooner settle his head on Ursula's breasts than be thrashed as the shuttlecock between practised gamesters.

'Do you know what you'll paint? The subject matter?' Ursula.

'No.'

'Nudes with pubic hair. That's what Arabs like.' Quinn.

'You've questioned a good many of them, I suppose.' Her sarcasm wasted itself.

When Worth had finished his cup of tea and Ursula had

22

found he did not want another, she ordered him out. He followed her to her bedroom, where she mothered him into the one armchair. The table, draped with an old-fashioned, tasselled, crimson cloth, was littered with exercise books she had been marking. Otherwise the room was tidiness itself; the single bed foursquare to the corner, the dark carpet sedately matching drawn curtains, the muffin walls rich with pictures. At the centre of the largest space hung a Worth watercolour, a long picture of an ash tree in winter, the bole a stunning green, and round it garden walls, a great straggling holly bush, the subdued purple rectangles of houses, a mist of shrubs and distant apple boughs. He looked at it, with approbation.

'Admiring the masterpiece?' she said, smiling on her chair, swinging her legs like a girl let out of school.

'Yes. Wouldn't do it like that again, though.'

'No,' she said, 'no.'

He gave her an account of the Burden Gallery, then of Walden, and their trip round the mansion.

'You didn't like him, did you?'

'No. Too assured for me. I like rough edges. Nerves.'

'How old was he?'

'Couldn't tell. Anything between sixty and eighty. Well preserved, but I'd guess near the higher limit.'

'What was wrong with him? Come on, man.'

'I'd never heard of him, and yet he seemed a big noise. They've done two exhibitions of my stuff, and I've never seen him before. I wonder if the Burdens haven't been taken over by some financiers, or television company, and he was their man. Don't know. He made out he was an art expert.'

'Was he?'

'How can you tell? There was no art lying about. And I didn't question him. I'm not interested enough.'

She sat on his knee, suddenly, and he absently stroked her legs, but the position was as awkward as he was tired, so that her father's bawling from the bottom of the stairs brought relief. She clattered down to answer the telephone, and once she was out of the way her father made his way up.

'She'll be half an hour on that damn' thing if I know her,' he

23

said, closing the bedroom door behind him. He jerked his head upwards, sideways, downwards like a dud amateur actor; man inspects premises. Worth waited for the comment on comfort, was disappointed. 'Seen that friend of yours today. Turnbull.'

'What was he doing?'

'Drivin'. Up Mapperley Street with a young woman.'

'That would be his wife.'

'Didn't look more than twenty.' Worth did not even glance up politely. 'I can remember him playing rugby. Name was often in the paper. Schoolmaster, isn't he?' The long *a* snarled envy. 'Lived up Grange Avenue, didn't he? At one time? Funny-looking chap; got legs like tree trunks. And you say that's his wife?'

'I didn't see her.'

'Young. Fair hair. Might have been wearing glasses.' He waited. 'I like women in glasses. Very attractive. But you can't get our Ursula wearing hers. Don't suppose you knew she had 'em, did you? Had headaches at college, few years back. Told her to get a pair for reading.'

'You did?'

'The doctor. At the college.' He picked up a pencil case, opened it and fiddled with the crayons, whistling no tune, drum-and-fife rhythm. 'Been better recently. Soon after her mam died.' He paused for a question. 'That'll be five years, six in October.' His sadness was foxy, malicious. They could hear Ursula's clumping ascent, the creak of the balustrade as she turned the corner.

'What are you doing here?' she asked her father. He dropped the crayons.

'I'm entertaining Man o' the Trees.'

'I like it,' Worth said.

'Well, you have painted rather a lot,' Quinn smirked, 'you'll admit.' He withdrew, pleased with life, and Ursula sat down hard.

'It's my lucky day. I've won a bottle of whisky in a raffle,' she said. 'They've been trying to trace me since Christmas. I've to collect it over in Sherwood. I don't drink whisky.'

'Give it to him.'

24

'I'd as soon pour it down the sink.'

They talked desultorily for a quarter of an hour, touched hands, kissed, but both were listless.

'You go home now,' she ordered. 'I'll finish these.' She pointed at the exercise books, moved purposefully across, not accompanying him downstairs. He turned lights on and off, for himself, donning coat and scarf, called out to Quinn who sagged into the hallway.

'You're off, then? Didn't she come down with you? Bloody women. Nothing suits sometimes. I'll bolt the door after you.' He did not bend to draw it, left that to the visitor. 'Turnbull. I've never spoken to him. He must be all of fifty.'

'How do you know of him?'

'Rugby. Photo was always in the paper at one time. Has he got children?'

'Two.'

'I sometimes wonder . . .' He had opened the door; an icy draught seemed instantaneously to numb their ankles. Worth did not wait; Quinn did not mind.

4

Worth had sketched hard for five days.

Quinn's jibe challenged him to draw trees, and he had dashed down a night-dark double line by a railway track seen from above, a splash of yellow sodium light bursting in the distance over a second bridge. One sketch was grandiose, two feet odd by eighteen inches, and pleased him, but it would only darken that elegant wall. Next he lashed colour about on a country fair in a field, the sky blue, small clouds fluffy, trees banished to mere miniature shapes beyond the booths, the gaudy, small roundabouts of prancing cockerels and horses, the roaring children, the big-booted men, perambulators, lolloping dogs, scared squadrons of birds. Now he turned to an urban landscape, the play of light on warehouses, on the clouds massing from the towers of a power station, on roofs by the hundred, main roads, on the holes and corners of gardens and their darkening walls, shadows, the random gleam of windows. No men walked there, no cars, but one felt them below the surface, burrowing or buried under the variations of paint.

At the end of his stint, five o'clock on Sunday evening, he looked again, interested himself, but was no longer convinced he had done anything to attract the customer. As he moved from painting to painting, he seemed to have opted for choices that would necessarily be rejected, and then to have worked himself into a lather making them memorable. Walden would turn them down, for certain, and would hate himself if he knew anything about art. Worth enjoyed the thought, cancelled it as self-inflating fantasy.

He ate his tea, sandwiches again, washed dishes, and considered walking the cold streets to pass an hour. As a gesture towards civilization, he bathed, changed into a suit, chose a matching shirt and tie. A pair of shoes decorously polished lay ready in the wardrobe. As he sat on his bed, in stockinged feet, the doorbell rang so that he had to search again for discarded slippers.

A girl in the half-light, well back from the door.

'Mr Worth.' He did not recognize the voice. 'My husband sent me to invite you round.' An awkward hiatus. 'I'm Millicent Turnbull.'

'Come in.'

'I've got the car.' A gleam of excited teeth and glasses as she passed him and pulled hard at her headscarf. 'Teddy said you'd be working yourself to death, and I wasn't to take no for an answer.' She sounded childishly elated, but wooden, as if repeating a set pattern of words. 'Will you come?'

'Where are we going?'

'To our place.'

'I'll consider it. I'll need to find my shoes.'

She sat with hands clasped round her knee and leaned forward like a child at a conjuring show, not quite believing her eyes.

'You've got a studio,' she said. 'Teddy's told me.'

'I'll show you over it. It's too cold tonight.'

'Thank you. I'd like that.'

'You don't come from these parts?'

'No, Farnham. That's where my father retired from the army. I was here at the Poly, doing law, but I gave it up. But I could type so I found a job. I don't think I'd be welcome back home. I've never tried.'

'Don't you write or phone?'

'Not much. There's no need. I mean, they don't want to hear. What can I say?'

'Do they know you're married?'

'Oh, yes. I wrote to them. I even invited them up. It only made bad worse.'

'And you're not sorry about this?'

'No. I never consider it. I suppose I ought, but I don't. We were never very,' she waved long, pale fingers, 'close. My dad was posted here, there and everywhere, and I had to change schools and friends. Don't think I'm complaining; I'm not. Plenty of others fared worse.'

'I don't know why I'm questioning you,' Worth said. 'I've no right.'

'I don't mind. I like it. It's friendly. And I can see your pictures. Just sitting here, and learning what your house looks like, and thinking I can perhaps come again is very good. Teddy's friends are conventional, really.'

'And I'm not?' He laughed at her scared expression.

'You haven't shown me the stair-carpet, or the kitchen fittings, or talked about grouting the tiles. Not that I'd run people down for that. Daddy was marvellous at home improvement, and so is Teddy. They would have been happier as plumbers or joiners.'

'Your husband always seemed very good at school.'

'I'm sure he is, but he isn't happy. He and the headmaster don't see eye to eye, and he thinks he does all the work. And, of course, he's got me. It does trouble him. I don't want any children; honestly, I don't, but I can see him looking at me, and wondering. And then Piers gets on his nerves. He hates the name for a start; his first wife chose it. Piers Michael Whalley Turnbull.' She laughed, rather nervously Worth thought, withdrawing herself from the offered confidences. 'This house isn't like you at all; the furniture's so solid and solemn.'

He grimaced comical doubt.

'It's Victorian, and some Edwardian. No veneer. Dovetail joints.' Though the room where they sat was large enough, with ceilings higher by two feet than modern equivalents, the sideboard, the glass-fronted bookcase floor to cornice, the table and six matching chairs seemed to demand something more ample.

'I hope you don't mind my saying this.'

'Why should I? It belonged to my mother, and her family before her.'

'You were an only child?'

'Yes.'

'Snap. I don't know if that's good or not. Teddy says you left teaching because you made some money with a cartoon strip.'

'I should have given up anyway. I'm unsuited to instruction.' He giggled. 'But Miriam and Victor came along conveniently, by luck and knowing the right body. It's still running. I spend one whole day every week at least at it. Miriam's a girl. Victor's her dog.'

'Animals are difficult to draw, aren't they?'

'No. I've never found it so. But this creature has to have a human expression. He smiles and frowns and leers. He's undoggy. It's a kind of trick and not too hard when you've once got it. I resent the time I spend on the thing now, but it's still syndicated in the north, and the man who planned it, and writes it, needs the money, and I feel superstitiously grateful so I work at it, and do it conscientiously, the art man's burden, under a pseudonym. Anyhow, it keeps me off the trees.'

'I'm afraid I don't follow you.'

'Don't you think I spend too much time painting them?'

'No. I hadn't noticed. Now you mention it, there are trees in some of your pictures. Why do you say that?'

'Just something somebody said to me.'

'And that worries you. I don't think Mozart would have

28

cared if somebody had told him he used too many crotchets.'

Worth shook his head at this illogicality, but she smiled and touched the tabletop.

'Why does your husband send you round tonight particularly?'

'He told me about this commission of yours. And he said he knew what you'd be like.'

Without hurrying, Worth outlined his labour over the last five days and explained why he thought he had wasted his time.

'Tomorrow,' he promised, 'I shall do what they want. Arthurian knights in purples and crimsons and greens. I'll do what they ask a couple of times, and then I'll please myself putting great black lines round the figures and melting the stained glass . . .'

'Melting?'

'Misshaping, distorting. I have to prove to myself that I'm my own man.'

'You don't like all this, do you?' Her voice seemed clear as water.

'Why do you say that?'

'The way you talk. I can tell you'd sooner be, well, at something else.'

'No,' he said. 'That's wrong. It does artists, especially conservative, academic painters like me, good to accept commissions that are right out of our line, or at least to try them. What we mustn't do is to substitute slickness for real advance. And it's harder to distinguish than you think. I'm prone to self-deception when I quit known boundaries. It's not so much the techniques, nor application, slog, it's the use they're put to. It's very difficult to say precisely what I'm driving at.' He knotted his forehead and his fingers crept aimlessly about the air. 'Let's say I twist or dispense with perspective, then I must replace it with what is its equivalent, and that means emotionally as well as aesthetically, in the particular picture.'

'You talk like a philosopher,' she said, round-eyed and impressed.

'Like a fool. I'll get my shoes on.'

She drove her old Ford fast and efficiently, like Walden in the Volvo, so that he wondered why he had thought she would be nervous. Once, tearing up a badly lit, cobbled side street, she laughed out loud and, stopping violently at the top, banged her gloved hands on the steering wheel in exhilaration.

The windows of the Turnbull house in Grange Avenue were dark and Millicent needed to unlock the front door. Inside she called out to her husband, but there in coolish silence the two stood, unanswered. She yodelled again, shyly taking Worth's arm in a cramped hall which smelled of roast beef and raincoats. They listened, to nothing.

'Even the heating's turned itself off,' she grumbled, feeling out to a radiator.

'Has he gone out?'

'The off-licence, I expect.' She seemed ill at ease.

'Why should he do that?'

'Hospitality.' She had let go his arm and made her way to the kitchen, kicking, by the sound, a pile of saucepans. 'That's switched the heating on,' she called. 'Don't take your coat off yet.' He stood in the hall, wondering whether or not he was expected to join her, when the front door banged open to admit Turnbull.

'Hello,' he shouted. 'Reception committee. You've beaten me to it. Where's Milly?'

'In here,' she answered the loud inquiry, cheerfully.

'Take your coat off,' Turnbull ordered.

'Don't you,' she called. 'Not till it's warmed up. You let it go off. It's like a morgue.'

'Never touched it.'

'You should have done.'

Turnbull struggled out of his sheepskin coat, but appeared no less square, broad by so doing. He picked up his bag, jangling bottles, and with his left hand opened the sitting-room door, turned on lights.

'Like a bloody music hall,' he complained. 'Go on in there.'

Worth obeyed, stood by the fireplace down which the wind rattled. In the kitchen Millicent and her husband were laughing, moving, noisily as if they were wearing clogs to shift

30

coal. The drawing room formed a large rectangle, but the effect of size only added to the shabbiness of the faded carpet, worn and in one place holed, the scuffed furniture, the chipped paint. The wall opposite the wide, black reflecting windows was decorated with an elegantly patterned paper, originally perhaps a dark green, but now almost as grey as the other walls, which had once been white. A patch above the picture rail near the curtains was peeling into an exploding rose eighteen inches across. The ornate gilt frame of a large shadow-dark oil painting was rustily discoloured, and upcurved moustaches stained the walls at the ends of the radiators. The whole room was seedy, spoke neglect; books on the yellowing open shelves zigzagged, were piled haphazardly, some upright, some flat, three with spines backward while about the floor were heaps of magazines, geographical, geological, all grubby. Yet on no surface was there any trace of dust; Worth dragged his fingers along the high, unsavoury, cold, metal mantelpiece to test his observation. The lights lacked power, shadowing and dimming.

Millicent bustled in to drag the curtains across. They, too, had been green.

'I don't know why he's brought you in here,' she said, returning. 'It's a real bachelor's midden. This is my first really big job, to redecorate this place. I've done the necessary measuring. I know what I want, and as soon as he carts his books out I shall start. All repainted; new curtains; new carpet; a chandelier. I've actually bought that. And I keep telling him, the longer he delays, the higher the cost. But he's so sluggish.' She looked at Worth wide-eyed. 'He's not usually. I think there's something psychological about this. He and Piers lived like pigs. Or it's his memorial to Elspeth,' his first wife, 'a dirty patch in his past life.'

'What the hell are you telling him now?' Turnbull from the door.

'That the state of this room expiates your adultery.'

'Balls.'

She laughed, hysterically, caught showing off. Her husband barged away somewhere outside while she knelt to the antiquated gas fire, which she lit fearfully from a match.

'This could be a beautiful room,' she said from her knees. 'Will you tell him to shift his rubbish? Then I'll lock myself in here, weekends and free evenings, and brighten the place up. I'll transform it. I bought a lock to put on the door, all brass. It'll be a present.'

'Will he be pleased?'

'As long as I pay for it out of my own pocket. He's mean with his money.' She laughed again. 'You think I shouldn't talk about him like that, don't you? It's not a bad fault, because he has to lob out to Elspeth. That's why all the lights were off when we came in. He was saving a penny.'

Worth, taken aback by the naïve frankness of the girl, looked down on her back, at her red fingers spread to the fire, which spluttered. He had never been in this room before, and felt disturbed by her talk, her presence, the wretchedness of the furnishings.

'You're very quiet,' she said, not looking up, and he confirmed it with silence. 'Teddy likes me to talk. In fact he likes pretty well everything I do because it's so different from Elspeth.' She turned to look up at him, cheeks glowing. 'He believes in Santa Claus now.'

'How do you like it in here, then?' Turnbull, arriving without fuss.

'Your wife's keeping me entertained.'

'She's hogging the gas fire. I can see that.'

Millicent scrambled to her feet, shaking out her hair, somehow breathless with unnoticed activity, and finally skipping to put an arm round part of her husband's waist.

'Elspeth ran off with all the decent furniture,' she said, 'even the carpet. This thing,' she kicked the wreck under her feet, 'had been out in the garden shed.'

'We don't need the place,' Turnbull said. He looked out of character standing entangled with the young woman, seemed relieved to turn out the fire and lead the party into the dining room where he offered his guest beer, coffee or tea.

'You've seen our disgrace now,' she said. The men drank coffee but she held up a glass of beer with bravado, congratulating her husband on the inch of foam into which she plunged her lips. Worth, pleased at her independence, offered them his now polished account of the London venture.

'And what's the position?' Turnbull.

'I've done some sketches, and I shall do some more.'

The Turnbulls sat tongue-tied, but their room was warm, bright, friendly. Suddenly all three began to talk together, stopped in concert and laughed uproariously, the host slapping his thighs.

'Your turn,' he said, pointing at Worth.

'Oh, nothing,' he mumbled. 'I wasn't really saying anything important.'

'I wish I was good with my hands,' Millicent said, without invitation.

'How's your pottery?' Worth asked her.

'Hilarious. Knotty.'

'You'd like,' Turnbull pronounced, 'to turn these London boys down, wouldn't you?'

'Not really.'

Millicent was watching him as if he'd come out with some world-shaking aphorism. Her husband gripped his chin between thumb and forefinger as he nodded his head so enormously that the roll of fat on his neck bulged and wrinkled. In the street the movement would have attracted a small crowd.

'How's Ursula?' Turnbull asked, giving up.

'I saw her the other night.' Millicent. 'She didn't see me. She doesn't know me.'

'She's fine. Her father saw the pair of you. He's an admirer of yours, he says, from your rugby days.' Turnbull was now cleaning out the bowl of his pipe with a key-shaped object, as noisy as it was efficient. He tapped a stream of charcoal dust into the ashtray, and blew down the stem.

'You're not going to smoke that, surely,' Millicent said.

'I am.' Husband and wife regarded each other with affectionate, reciprocal congratulation.

'You'll die too soon,' she said.

'For what?' He dug out of his pocket a yellow oilskin pouch, which he opened. He rubbed tobacco in his palm, not minding their scrutiny, in this at least perfectly sure of himself. Nobody spoke again until the room drifted with his smoke.

The girl laughed, throwing her legs about, as she described the office where she worked, and then Turnbull, doggedly puffing at his pipe, muttered his way through the latest altercation with his headmaster. Each enjoyed the other partner's turn; one silently, one with vivacity. Next they confessed that they had joined a ballroom dancing class, but in spite of his wife's encouragement Turnbull refused to stand and demonstrate his skill.

'I've two left legs,' he grumbled.

'On the contrary,' she said, 'like a good many weighty people he's very light on his feet.'

Worth inquired where they'd practise the skill once they'd acquired it, and was impressed by their knowledge, and the amplitude of opportunity.

'I tell you this,' Turnbull said, plopping at his pipe stem, 'I wish I'd learnt years ago.'

'Elspeth was against it.' Millicent.

'It never occurred to us. We'd as soon have gone high-diving or dirt-track racing.' He laughed to himself. 'We did try skiing. Couple of times.'

'And?' Worth.

'Good tan. We weren't so bad. But then the kids came.'

'Don't say that,' Milly objected. 'I like to hate Elspeth.'

'Elly and Milly,' Worth said. The others pointedly ignored him. Turnbull began to recall Continental trains and frontier difficulties, ending with the rescue of some Cambridge lady don from a ticklish financial perplexity at an out-of-the-way Austrian railway station. Worth had difficulty in understanding the details, but Millicent seemed rapt.

'I wasn't even born,' she said. At this Turnbull puffed harder.

Between them they kept Worth occupied with their talk, for they delighted in each other. If one approached embarrassing topics, the other blushed, smoked, grunted or kept silent, giving the impression that something better would make an almost immediate appearance. Worth enjoyed this, for neither partner was tactful, but each had enough zest for the other's company and conversation to avoid giving hurt. This was love.

The thought of the two rolling naked in bed invited his derision, but this social, pleasurable duet, which he found he had not expected, moved him. There was something of the circus about it, slightly ramshackle, as if the coloured boards would be transplanted tomorrow, with tyre-marked mud and a scatter of sawdust all that was left of the late brilliance, the breathtaking impossibilities.

Millicent was no slave of her husband, and dominated the conversation. Her final feat was to take on both men with the threat that when Worth went to London to execute his commission, she'd demand a week, or more, of owed holiday to transform the sitting room.

'How long will this mural occupy you?' she asked.

'They won't offer me the chance.'

'You must make them. Otherwise we shall live in squalor.' She pointed at her husband. 'On the day Mr Worth gets the go-ahead, you'll clear those shelves, won't you?'

'If you say so.'

'And move the furniture out?'

'Yes.'

'You heard him, Mr Worth. Now it's up to you.'

They did not quite manage to laugh; they joked as if they did not see a reason, as if fear hovered. Worth felt put out and, not sorry to leave, said he'd walk home.

5

It took Worth a further week to complete his sketches, which he dispatched at once to the gallery. There followed the expected silence after the briefest note of acknowledgement, so that even as he continued to occupy himself he begrudged the time he had wasted on the work. Late one evening, at the moment when he had returned from a walk round the streets, Walden had telephoned him.

The voice sounded old, delicate and very foreign. 'Mr Worth. I have been trying for the last hour to contact you. I have shown your sketches to our client, and he does not like them.'

Worth did not answer that, stared in distaste through an open kitchen door revealing saucepans in lines, hanging culinary utensils, a teatowel, tureens.

'Did you hear me?' the exotic voice probed.

'Yes.'

'This is a disappointment. For me as well as you.' Worth pulled faces. 'Can you hear me? The line seems bad.'

'I can.'

'We must consider our next move.'

'Send the sketches back.'

'I cannot hear you very well.'

'Send them back.'

'But Mr Worth, Mr Worth.' Walden seemed alarmed; one could see his fragile claws raised heavenward. 'We must not look on it like that. This is just the beginning of negotiations. We must talk, must find out. The gentleman is used to inquiry, and bargaining. He will not understand blunt negatives, immediate blockages any more than I do.'

Worth made no reply.

'I have talked to him,' Walden continued, 'helped him to understand in terms of painting what it is he wants.'

'Am I the only iron in the fire?'

'The only artist? I see. No, you are not. You are the one I expect to land the commission. The favourite.' He chuckled, thin as tissue paper, presumably at his racing term. 'But, no, there are others.'

'Right.'

'Competition should act as a spur. This is something to be brought to a conclusion, to a triumph.'

'Send the sketches back.' Gall seethed.

'That is, if I may say so, Mr Worth, not very enterprising. Completion will bring in a considerable monetary reward. Considerable. But I need to convince the client.'

'What does he know about it?'

'He is not ignorant. He is a cultured man. But he leans, to some extent, on my advice. He has trusted me in other transactions. In this case I cannot put forward my full powers of persuasion because I am not myself convinced.'

'Of what?' Worth enjoyed boorishness.

'That we have extended you to your full potential.'

'Look,' Worth said, 'you've got other people who want the commission more than I do. Extend them.'

'You're angry, Mr Worth. That is your disappointment. I have experience, and I have admired your work some years now. One of your Burwell paintings has pride of place in my sitting room. I am not trying, as you suspect, to demonstrate my power over you by giving or denying you this work. I think I know what I am about. Now, please listen. I will tell you what I have decided about your submissions.'

Very rapidly, obviously reading from notes, he outlined criticism of each of the sketches, one by one. In spite of the speed of delivery it took twenty-five minutes to complete the survey of the twelve paintings. Worth was impressed; the Sunday paper headings – composition, colour, technique, derivation – he had no time for, but Walden looked for something beside, the emotional derivation, the power latent, the odd word, intransigence of the art with the life on which it was based, the durability of the quality. What could easily have been pretentious word spinning spoke tellingly bare here.

'Now, Mr Worth, what do you think?'

'You have gone to some trouble.'

'That is so. I will always put myself out for someone like you. But what do you think of my conclusions?'

'I don't know whether they're right or not.'

'But are they wrong? Do they not have the ring of authenticity? Could you not see that I have sat down for hours with your work?'

'No.'

'Mr Worth, you are a difficult man.'

'I don't think so. But I'm a painter, and words don't mean much where pictures are concerned. If somebody thinks I've got it wrong, he should pick a pencil up and do it better.'

'That would not be easy over the telephone.' Walden was laughing softly, pleased with his wet wit; one could imagine his small teeth bared. 'But we should talk on, because I do not delude myself that I could show you how to do it.'

'Why do you want me? Why won't someone else do?'

'As soon as we were approached, I thought of you. You are capable, but you need stretching. You are an awkward man, and you need someone no less obstinate to commission you. You think that you know what you do best; I know that I shall test you, and you will be the better for it.'

Worth grunted; he felt the need of warm sheets.

'You needn't be afraid, Mr Worth. I am determined to make you better than you are. You do not like this. You do not need funny, foreign old men poking their noses in, because you think you are self-sufficient. But it is not so. You need me.'

Again Worth did not bother to answer.

'I will not drag you up to London. I will visit you. Do you agree to that?'

'Well . . .'

'Come, Mr Worth, you have nothing to lose. Will you agree?'

They fixed a date, and Worth found himself issuing travel instructions. His enthusiasm surprised him.

'That is, if I may say so,' Walden was purring, 'more like it. This is not going to be easy, and I do not claim it will be. I shall annoy you, Mr Worth, because you are, if I may be pardoned, worthy. You have the talent, but you are provincial, limited, easily satisfied with regard to the scope of your work. I shall enlarge you. You are young, but experienced as well as talented and this is the time to shift your ground. If you are to become an important artist, now is the moment to move. Don't you agree?'

Worth was both flattered and angry.

'If I'm going to be a great artist it will come of my own efforts.'

'To a large extent. But environment, luck, patronage, advice and criticism will play their part. I shall act.'

'What makes you think you can?'

'Self-conceit.'

They both laughed.

38

'I am not modest, Mr Worth, as you are. Go and tell your friends that a man is coming from London to make a great figure of you.' Silence. 'You don't say anything?' The conversation did not, could not, last much longer, but the painter was not displeased.

On the following day Worth invited Ursula Quinn round to judge and comment on Walden's proposal. She sat solemnly, blue-eyed, occasionally patting her raven-black hair, a glass of gin at her elbow.

'Sounds exciting,' she volunteered flatly, when she had heard him out.

'I can't make head or tail of the man.'

'Did he seem sane? Did he suggest how he was going to transform you into a genius?'

'By advice, or suggestion.'

'Do you believe he can?' she persisted.

'No.'

'Do you think you're a genius?'

'I've a high opinion of my capabilities, I'll tell you that. But if you think Walden can turn me into a Rembrandt or a Michelangelo, I don't. And if that's what he's claiming, then he's wrong.'

'You're a bit calm, aren't you?'

'Calm?'

'You're too settled, easy-going. You could do with going raving mad.'

'Would you,' he asked reasonably, 'be sitting here like this if I did?'

'But that's not the question.'

They talked on; Ursula was intrigued, mischievously so, and suggested that she should spend the Saturday when Walden visited him in the house, if only as cook for the day.

'That's trespassing on your good nature.'

'You talk like a fool.' He hated that; she had something of her father's malicious vulgarity. 'I'm curious. I want to see how he works the transfiguration. So I shall be there with my ha'penny.'

In fact, she arrived on the Friday evening before the visit and said she was staying the night.

'Not in your bed either. I've brought my sleeping bag and I shall doss down in the small room.'

'There's a bed made up, in the front.'

'He might need that.' She made him hump her three huge cases upstairs and then when she had laid out her mattress came down and produced menus. 'You'll be shopping first thing,' she said. 'It will give you something to do. I shall stay over Sunday if he does.'

'Does your father know you're here?' Worth asked, trying to recover ground, and breath.

'Yes.'

'And is he pleased about it?'

'No. He'll have to get his own meals.'

At ten o'clock she took a bath before retiring to the sleeping bag. She made it clear that sex was out, brooked no argument, had her mind directed elsewhere. Next morning, after a frugal breakfast, tea, toast, cheese and apples, and again he had no choice, she presented him with a list.

'Cross off what you've already got,' she ordered. He complied. 'Now have you the money to pay for those?'

'I've a chequebook.'

'Right.' She looked hard at him. 'I'm working on the assumption that Walden's staying tomorrow.' He returned no answer. 'If he does, so do I.'

When he returned, laden, puffing and blowing, she was sitting in a chair reading a magazine, with all her father's insouciance, except no cigarette drooped at her mouth. She checked the purchases and before she moved into the kitchen issued him with a duster and vacuum cleaner.

'Walden, from your account, will be a bit of an old woman so he won't like untidiness or dirt. Just square up, carefully. He'll be here at eleven-thirty, you say, and you can take him straight into the studio. I shall bring your coffee in, and you can do your talking in there. Lunch will be on the table at one-thirty.'

'What if he's late?'

'Everything goes back.'

'Don't I have any say in this?'

40

She stared at him as at a stupid pupil, sighed histrionically, shook her head impatiently as if she'd decided against answering before she said, flatly enough, 'I'm serious. That means I'm taking this man at his word. If he's a poseur, too bad. If he isn't you'll need two hours with him before lunch. I shall eat with you, and that should give you a rest. Then back to it or not, as you decide. But we'll give him his chance.'

Worth was impressed, went off to tidy his house, before she gave him his exeat at 10.45.

'Any instructions?' he asked, mockingly.

'You're a bloody fool.'

When Walden appeared, five minutes early, Worth, who had changed into a decent suit, opened the door and directed him to the studio. A quarter of an hour later Ursula carried in the coffee pot and cups, was briefly introduced to Walden who paid her no attention beyond a quick, rude appraisal and a limp handshake. The sketches were already laid out, and both men looked at them rather than at her in the minute she was in the room. At 11.45 she collected the tray and told them that lunch would appear at 1.30. Again, neither man took notice of her, but both seemed shifty, unnerved as if caught out in indecency. At twenty minutes past one she hammered on the studio door, ordered them to be ready for the meal.

'The bathroom's upstairs,' she informed Walden. He trotted away. She dragged Worth to the kitchen. 'How have you got on?' she asked, working still.

He made indeterminate humming noises at which she clashed her pans.

'What did he say?'

'Well, he told me what was wrong with my sketches.'

She waited; he did not explain further, but stood sulkily, not filling his suit.

'Have you learnt anything?'

'I suppose so.'

'You're going to annoy me before this day's out,' she warned, and turned her back. Walden reappeared, was led to the dining room, offered dry sherry. Worth, chastened, helped carry and serve the meal, soup, roast lamb, bread-and-butter

41

pudding, and though the visitor ate without enthusiasm he congratulated Ursula on the excellence of her cooking.

'What do you make of him?' she asked. Worth had gone out to provide coffee.

'He is talented.'

'Have you convinced him he should do what you say?'

'I would not claim that.'

'Why not?'

'My dear young lady,' the accent became preternaturally foreign and the face round it frozen, 'how can I tell? I am, like you, a human being.' He touched the wineglass from which he had drunk sparingly. 'I can only suggest.'

'Does he pay any attention?'

'Who is to say?'

'You are,' she burst out. 'That's why you're here, isn't it? You're the evangelist.'

'I don't know that,' he answered.

'You turned his sketches down. You claim you can make him come up with something worthwhile. Have you done so?'

'Why are you so interested? Tell me.' He spoke very gently.

'Because he's gifted. But he's too bloody slow. He'll go round dabbing bits of leaves and bark on canvas until he's a hundred if you let him.'

'Why,' Walden leaned right back in his chair lifting the front legs from the carpet and spoke towards the ceiling, 'don't you do something about it? Yourself?'

'I know nothing about art. If I started on it, what could I say to him? Liven yourself up. But what then? Go and paint war pictures. But for all I know, cavalry charges can be just as dull as tree trunks.'

'Possibly. It is possible. Do you love him?'

'No. Not really.'

'Why are you here, then? Do you live here?' She shook her head. 'Did he ask you? To be his servant, cook his meals?'

'No, I told him I was coming. So that I could see you.'

Walden rubbed his little belly; he now sat straight upright, like a puppet.

'I shall try not to disappoint you. The trouble is that he has not been marked enough by the world.'

42

'He was going to marry a girl and she committed suicide.'

'For what reason?'

'I've no idea. He does just talk about her. Sometimes. She was older than he was. I think he'd known her since he was a boy. But there seemed to be no compelling reason. He was away on holiday at the time, painting, and she took an overdose.'

'Was he in any way connected with the event?'

'I've no idea.'

'Could one mention this to him, do you think?' He cocked a devilish eye at her. 'Could I? Would that . . . ?' He broke off, stared beyond the room, the beautiful fingers still meddling with the wineglass, the glassy, small shoes together. Ursula knew she had said enough, but was disappointed that Walden had not spoken with more authority. As he sat, he was a tiny, grey man, a mouse, quick and cunning but worryingly weak. He abandoned the glass to stroke his chin.

When Worth brought in the coffee, the three sipped in silence, embarrassed, failing to glance, to catch glances.

'Off you go.' Ursula tried to sound hearty. 'Get on with whatever it is you're going to do.'

'I'll help you with the dishes,' Worth protested.

'Mr Walden has not come here to watch you wash pots.'

'Wash pots,' Walden mused. 'Pots.'

She applied herself energetically in the kitchen, dealing with the dinner things, cleaning the stove, before she bleached his sink, reorganized his comestibles. It pleased her to sing, "With verdure clad", her head spinning with the beauty of the music, as her hands scoured and rattled. She finished the wine, a half-glass of hock, and heard nothing of the men. At 4.15, after she had taken to the gas fire in the sitting room, Worth burst in.

'Mr Walden's going now.'

Ursula straightened the skirt of her dress, followed him out to the hall where Walden had already donned his overcoat. He held smart, pale gloves in his left hand.

'I'm pleased to have met you,' he announced.

'Have you had a successful day?' she asked.

'That remains to be seen. We have begun to talk. Let's put it like that. I think he understands me that little bit better.'

He stuck out his right hand militarily – he ought to have

clicked heels – and, valediction over, pulled on his gloves like an officer on parade. Worth accompanied him to the front gate.

She had filled the kettle when he returned, and he propped himself by the sink, unspeaking, apparently at a loose end. After she had poured large mugs of tea, she refused to sit in the front room. They drank, uncomfortably.

'Aren't you going to say anything?' she demanded.

'There's not much I can say.'

'Was he any good?'

'I think he was. He was as good as anybody like that could be. But what does that mean?'

'Has he done anything for you?'

He shrugged, and his hands groped in front of him, like a blind man's.

When she said she'd go upstairs to pack he took her in his arms, but she stood unresponsive, not struggling, not quite ignoring him but on guard, waiting for the password.

'I'm shocked,' he said. 'Frightened.'

'Go on.'

'He was good on individual pictures, what he said, you know. And he made some rum suggestions. "Be brutal." He told me to make sketches of the cherry blossom when it comes out and put some rotting corpses under the trees.'

'You don't want to do that?'

'What do you think? His line was always this: Do you want to go on painting trees and hills for local exhibitions in the Castle Museum? If you do, is it because you're a pretty little dauber, or do you believe these provincial bits and pieces play a huge part in the wide world? It happens, he said. Sometimes, rarely, some little man makes his hole-and-corner miniature concerns important, but only when and because the demon inside him runs blazing, searing, torturing hot. He asked which sort I was.'

'And what did you say?'

'Nothing. I pulled a face at him. At home.'

She hugged him to her and they hurried upstairs to make love, but when that was over, she packed her cases, refusing to stay an hour more. She offered no advice.

44

6

When next morning, Sunday, the Turnbulls invited him over, pressed for a report of Walden's visit, Worth felt bound to speak honestly, with bravado.

'He told me to tell all my friends that he'd come from London to make a great painter of me.'

They looked at him, round-eyed, suspiciously cautious.

'That's marvellous,' Millicent said in the end.

'It's only talk,' he answered her, but at her stricken look he described the greenish corpses under the flowering cherry he'd been instructed to paint.

'Will you do it?'

'Don't know about that. I can't help feeling he's right. That whereas I'd be content to try to reproduce, never so successfully as in actuality, what the nature of the blossom is, I ought to push myself, not because there's anything wrong with dabbling with reality except one soon becomes satisfied with an approximation that is better than others are managing but not by much. As soon as one introduces the corpses, death by politics or passion, one needs, one sees rather, more than mere craftsman-like prettiness.'

'I think I understand that,' Millicent whispered.

'If you ask me, he's typical of your London extremist pervert,' Turnbull blustered. 'Art doesn't consist of an imitation nowadays of a man getting himself a meal, he has to cut his own testicles off and fry them up for his breakfast. That's madness. It's the power of the imitation that counts.'

'Except that some subjects seem to exact more, stimulate the imagination more violently.'

'Only when your imagination's jaded. When Rembrandt draws a back-garden fence it's as miraculous as anybody else's *Rape of the Sabine Women*.'

45

Millicent perked up, delighted with her husband.

'You sound quite cross,' she said.

'Why shouldn't I be?'

'You've never said anything about art before.'

He playfully slapped her bottom.

'Will you paint the corpses?' she asked.

'Of course he will. That's the only way to find out.'

'Headless corpses,' she mused.

'Why did you say that?' her husband, forcefully, eyes bulging.

'I don't know.'

'You see how you're misleading the young, now?' Worth did not know whether the man spoke seriously or not.

They argued in a way both desultory and angry, as if she, they, were all uncertain what or how to think, but when the painter rose to leave, Millicent put her hand on his sleeve.

'Don't forget,' she said, 'that when you start on your commission, I begin on our black hole.' She pointed at Turnbull. 'That means you'll have to clear your old rubbish out.'

'Two of us,' Worth answered.

'You haven't got the bloody job yet.' Turnbull ground his toe into the carpet, and his wife tripped away to the kitchen.

That afternoon Millicent rang Worth from a call box, asking if she could come round. She sat primly on the settee, but pert of face, as if excited.

'I just phoned on impulse. We had a row, over dinner. Natalie was supposed to appear, but didn't turn up, and that narked him because we kept waiting and waiting. Then he got on again about your commission and bloody lunatics and perverts. I pulled his leg; it takes him out of himself, usually. I said he didn't want his sitting room decorated, that it was his Bluebeard's Castle, and all the rest, but he only got angrier. I know when he's really cross because he's very quiet, and his lips are thin, and he chews at them with his top teeth.'

'I'm sorry. I'm the cause of all this.'

'I don't think so. I can't make it out, really. I think he knows he ought to have done something about that room long enough ago, and he's ashamed now that he hasn't. As I see it, it doesn't matter, but not Teddy. He's not very well, you know.'

'What's wrong with him?'

'Blood pressure. He's worried about Natalie.'

'Is she getting a divorce?'

'No, she's talking about a reconciliation with her husband.'

'And he thinks that's not on?'

'He was against the marriage in the first place. But you knew that. I quite like him, Alan, that is. He's got a lot about him. And he's making money. Teddy thought he was a fool to throw up teaching, but it's paid off. And Piers is a bother. His doctorate's going all right, he says, but he stands no chance of a university job when it's done. Ted worries about it. And the school gets him down.' All her liveliness had disappeared so that she sat pallid and he noticed for the first time that she had not removed her coat. 'I don't know why I'm telling you all this, except you seem to be connected. You've got to drag yourself out of your bolthole, that man said. And so has he.'

'I should have thought you'd have done that for him.'

She shook her head, at ridiculous length. 'Sometimes he regrets he's married me.'

'Why do you say that?'

'He's conservative. He lives in the past. My father was a raver compared with him, and he spent all his life in the army. I think, sometimes, that he hankers after Elspeth again, and remembers when Piers and Natalie were young and he could mend their toys or take them out in a pushchair.'

'You're a sharp young woman.'

'I wish I was. I feel so awful after something like today's row, because I don't know what to do or what to say.'

'Does it happen often?'

'Not really. But sometimes he worries that he'll die and leave me to fend for myself.'

'Aren't you capable of that, then?'

'As anybody else.' She laughed, nervously. 'He thinks that his children despise him or laugh at him because he married me.'

'And do they?'

'Possibly,' Millicent replied, clutching the cloth of her coat by her ribs. 'Piers is self-centred, but even he must consider his mother, and think that she had a rough deal.'

'Do they visit her?'

'As far as I know. They don't say anything to me, of course.'

She sat, knees together, pale-faced, a momentarily dull girl, a whipped child.

'I had to tell somebody. I felt so awful. I came out of the way, for a walk.'

'Will he have recovered by the time you go back?'

'I hope so. I don't know. Sometimes I dread that he'll have done something silly.' She giggled, or so it sounded. 'No, he won't, though. He's not really like that.' She stared into his eyes. 'Will you paint those corpses under the blossom?'

'Maybe.'

'That's what we're talking about now, isn't it?'

'Come again.'

'Life isn't pretty. Not all the time. Not even most of the time. Pictures hang on walls, and we look at them, but they shouldn't rest us, should they? They should prepare us, and strengthen us. Because there'll be blows, and deaths, and divorces.'

'I don't know,' Worth said. 'I suppose that's about it.'

'You should know. You're an artist. And that's not just a man who can draw or handle paint or design, he's somebody who's opening life out to us. That's what this Walden man is telling you.'

'And what if I don't want to know it?'

'You'll be a failure. Even if you're a dazzling technician you'll be third-rate.' She stood up, bristling, her fists clenched, breathing rapidly.

'Where do you get these ideas from?' he asked.

'Is there something wrong with them, then?'

'You're young. You ought to be worrying about the colour or price of your next dress, not the sorrows of the wide world.'

'That's typical of a man. I'm a married woman, with responsibilities. I'm not just a pretty doll Teddy's acquired to look well about the place.'

'I'm sorry.'

48

She dropped her head and then, surprisingly, stepped across to him, laid her cheek on his chest and her hands on his shoulders. They stood thus, silently, and he gently embraced her with his right arm, stroking her shoulder bones. He smelt her hair, recently shampooed; her breasts plagued him. He kissed the top of her head.

'You shouldn't have done that,' she whispered.

She had broken away, but only to a yard's distance; her eyes were tight shut.

'Sex,' she said. 'Sex, sex.'

'Better than headless corpses.' He tried to justify himself, unjustifiably.

'I wasn't a virgin,' Millicent said, 'when I married Teddy. I'd been living with a student at college, but we broke it up. That's why I left. Or partly. Law was boring, but I couldn't concentrate, neither on that nor anything else I was so unhappy. So I took a job. My parents didn't understand, but then I didn't expect them to. My life was a raw mess. I took up with another man, very shortly, and that was no good, either. It was a pleasure to go to the office and type letters and take shorthand and phone calls. It numbed me; it was all I was fit for. I hated everything; men, and mummy's letters. Daddy came up, paid me a surprise visit, but he didn't know what to say. What could he? He tried to get me to go back with him. He tried to give me money. I saw he was frightened and stupefied and dumb, because he wanted a daughter like everybody else's, who did well in exams, and wore nice dresses, and loved her pony, and married a stockbroker.'

'Didn't you want to please him?'

'No. I wanted to drag him down in the mud with me, and daub his collars with it. My God, I felt so ill.'

'Is that when you met Teddy?'

'Not till later. I made myself sign up for a course that he took on the local background to industrial history. I thought I wanted classical gods and nymphs and fauns. Plashing about naked in the Pierian spring. Learning and Greek letters and poetry to act like drugs. But that was cancelled.'

'And it worked?'

'By that time I was coming round, anyway. We, the class, used to go out for a drink, and Teddy drove me home a time or two. And then we were off. He and Elspeth were in trouble without my help. They barely spoke except to quarrel over Natalie and Alan. And then he told her one night he was in love with me. He'd already told me but I couldn't believe it. She hit him. She picked up her big handbag from the table and hit him with it. He walked out and came round to my flat; it was early evening and he stayed till one in the morning.'

Millicent sat, wiping a wisp of pale hair from her forehead. 'She divorced him for adultery with me, and took all she could. He kept the house, she didn't like it, ever, he said, but he had to give her her share in cash. He'd nothing except what he earned, and there was Natalie sponging on him, and Piers still at Oxford.'

'How long have you been married now? A year, is it?'

'Thirteen months. And we're quarrelling already. That's terrible. Do you think I'm too young for him? I'm twenty-three years old.' She looked eighteen at the outside. 'I don't want him unhappy on my account. You didn't see him when they first split. It broke his heart, because he remembered what Elspeth was like when they first met and what he'd felt about her then. Or that's what I thought. Perhaps what he didn't like was all the upset; he didn't want change and court appearances.'

'As long as I've known him, he'd speak out for what he thought was right.'

'But he didn't know here, did he? He wasn't right, was he? He kept asking me how a decent man could desert an ageing woman who needed him. Elspeth could make him feel guilty as hell. Though she didn't want him, and couldn't get on with him and was glad to get shot of him, she resented the fact I'd stolen her husband, and she'd a biting tongue.'

'Would they have broken up even if you hadn't appeared?'

'That's what Elspeth said. She used to come round and curse and howl at me, and she shouted so. Not like an educated woman. A fishwife. And more than once she told me that if it hadn't been me it would have been some other piece with tits he could slobber over.'

50

'Is it true?' Why did he ask that?

'How can you tell? I don't know what to think. Even now, when it's all over and done with. I wanted some steady man to pat me on the head and encourage me and look after me, and he needed an escape from hell at home.'

'Were you surprised?'

'Surprised? What do you mean?'

'There's a great difference in your ages.'

'Twenty-seven years. That didn't matter because we were both in such trouble. You wouldn't worry about a bad complexion, let's say, if you were drowning, would you?'

'Didn't? Does it matter now?'

'Now? We stagger on from day to day. And he turns to his books and his school, and I tot up my figures and listen to loves and disasters in the typing pool. I've come crying to you, that's a new one, so that when I go home to Ted I shan't have any bad feeling left, and I'll make a fuss of him, and he'll like it, and we'll survive. For a bit longer.'

'You sound pessimistic.'

'Not particularly. I don't expect too much.'

They talked for perhaps ten minutes more, and he apologized that he had not offered her food and drink.

'I wanted an attentive ear,' she said.

There was a resilience about her, a core of obstinacy, that in no way suited his image of her, the pale child, the helpless hand stretched out. She would upend him and Turnbull and six others like them if it suited her book. She left the house suddenly; she stood, made for the door and let herself out, so that one minute they had appeared immersed in conversation, and the next the house was emptied of her presence. Odd.

He took out a small sketch-pad and drew her, upstairs alone, in a tilting bus, laughing, pointing, talking feverishly to nobody. That was less than satisfactory.

51

7

For the next weeks he worked violently for Walden, as sun grew stronger and blossom whitened the cherry, the pear trees in spite of east winds. Ursula nagged him, mocked, expressed a clowning surprise that the great painter heralded had not yet materialized. Her father had called round at the house, for the first time in his life, on a social visit; he had dressed for the part with black laced, cracked shoes and a trilby hat.

'I just thought I'd drop in,' he announced himself. Worth, who was wasting time with a catalogue, tried to look affronted. 'Our Ursula's been on about nothing else.' He received no encouragement. 'I've never been round an artist's studio.'

Worth led him to the unheated room where they saw two bare easels, a neatish bench, a second cleared work surface, and a large tabletop smeared with paint and half covered with newspaper.

'This is it, then,' Quinn mused. 'Don't you get smears and spots on the floor?'

'If I don't put something down.'

'These quarry tiles look well, but they're cold on the feet.'

'I see.'

Quinn took another turn round the room, stopping, rubbing his chin.

'You had the old copper took out,' he'd said, or 'This is a nice view of the garden. Didn't realize you'd got quite so much land. Now you come to think of it, there isn't any street behind you, is there? So you would have plenty. That stream'll run somewhere down there if I've got my bearings right.' Worth neither commented nor answered, but Quinn grinned cunningly, pleased with his intrusion, ignoring resentment. He began on a third exploratory tour, jingling the coins in his trouser pocket, and though he found nothing to say continued to talk.

'Very interésting,' he concluded. 'Very interésting indeed.' They emerged into the front passage where Worth made no attempt to introduce him to the other rooms. Quinn screwed his eyes, shoved both hands deeply into his trouser pockets, whistled no tune in particular. 'Our Ursula's been all on edge, ever since that man came from London.'

'Has she?'

'You should know. She's more likely to tell you things than me. But I said to her, plain John Blunt, he's only a man, when all's said and done.' He shifted his feet. 'She thinks this fellow'll change you, in some way. She's as good as said as much. I don't know if you're serious about her.' No answer vouchsafed, Quinn growled, 'Well, are you? Because I'll tell you this, she's set on you.' Nothing again, though rudeness was negated by Worth's earnest frown, his lip-licking attention. 'She's had young men before. There was one at college she was very fond of, used to bring him home; clever young chap he was. Brightest there, she said. Came to nothing, though. And she ditched him. Didn't come up to scratch in some way. But this last few weeks there's been no living with her.'

'Why's that?'

'You. And this London chap. And the picture. She's highly strung.'

'What makes you so sure it's what you say it is?'

'Can't be nothing else. Stands to sense.'

'I've hardly seen her.'

'You don't have to see anybody to worry about 'em, do you? You've not given her up, have you? Chucked her?'

'No. I've been busy.'

'She doesn't think you have, does she?' Aggression combined easily with obsequiousness.

'Not so far as I know.'

'You're a funny bogger. I don't rumble yer, I'll tell you straight.' Quinn who could speak grammatically, in standard English, when he chose, tightened his throat to convey plebeian puzzlement, dissatisfaction. 'She's a bag of nerves.'

'I thought she was exactly the opposite.'

'You thought wrong, then.' He bared his small teeth. 'I'll

give you a bit of advice. Look after yourself, number one.'

'Weren't you telling me just now to look after Ursula?'

'Ne'er you mind 'er. She's like her mam. Makes out she's dying, but'd have the shirt off your back. She knows which side her bread's buttered. Both.' He punched Worth, quite painfully, in the shoulder. 'But you don't want me mother-hardying here all day.'

He left, evidently satisfied with his mission, pausing in the garden to pull down crudely a branch to sniff orange berberis, and then to wave back as if he'd drawn attention to a significant symbol.

As Worth expected, Ursula telephoned that evening to ask if it were convenient to look in on him.

She had dressed carefully, soberly, in a navy and white coat, with a hat, and flawless tights. If she went to an interview for a new job, she'd doll herself up like this, and he'd appoint her a headmistress at once. To buttress his morale, he led her to the scullery rather than the sitting room, and they sat there, open biscuit tin between them, drinking instant coffee from mugs. She made efficient inquiries about his health, and let him understand that her father had spoken about his visit.

'What had he to say for himself?' she asked, briskly.

'Didn't he tell you?'

'I'd sooner hear your side of the story.'

He began and ended his modest narrative by raising his mug in an ironical toast.

'He came, you say, to warn you to take care of me and finished by advising you to look after yourself?' she said.

'That's so.'

'Typical.'

'Isn't that what he told you?'

'Not exactly. His view is that you're crafty, and need watching. Moreover, he's curious, if idle, and he wanted to see what your house was like.'

'Was he impressed?'

'By the size of your garden.'

They fenced like this for perhaps twenty minutes before she abruptly asked, 'Aren't you going to show me what you've been doing?'

'If that's what you want.'

'Why else should I come?'

'It'll be cold in the studio.'

She smacked her mug hard down on the metal draining-board, waiting for him to move.

His drawings were all largish, nearly three feet by one and a half, and hung together between black covers inside a cupboard. He laid them on the table, stood back.

'Open up,' she ordered. Reluctance slowed him.

The first two depicted a length of lawn, closely mown, leading to a border and fence, seen from under a bough of barely opened cherry blossom. In the first, the sky was blue and mildly disturbed by small, white flatnesses of clouds; in the second, great dumplings of cumulus dominated the upper third of the picture and part-darkened the grass. No humans were seen, either in the brightness or the incipient dimming of light.

'Well?' he said.

'Go on.' She did not keep disappointment out of her voice; these would have done for high-class advertisement of fertilizer or double-glazing. His mouth twitched, and he stood quite still, trousers shabbily low over his shoes. 'Go on,' she repeated.

The next sketch showed the same piece of ground but now the artist had retreated, the cherry bough diminished, less important, though drawn with detailed care, so that more of the tree, the bole slightly reddish, stood revealed. Above, the sky stretched cloudlessly blue and on the ground, consequently, shadows were black, sharp-edged in bright sunshine. One noticed these details only later, for in the foreground were the twisted backs of a firing squad, smoke thinly struggling upwards from the muzzles of their raised rifles. They wore an odd, soldierly headgear, Foreign Legion caps with grey protective cloth at the back hiding all identity, height and shoulder width only differentiating between them. At the other end of the garden – and a distortion, like that of a television camera, made it seem further off than in the other two pictures where perspective was treated more formally or normally – sagged the executed victim, hatless, hair raggedly combed, fastened in some way to a small post by hands pinioned behind his back, on his knees, chin on chest, grey, baggy suit unmarked by bullet-holes or blood.

She drew in breath, sharply. 'Hell,' she whispered, shaken, 'and hell's bells.'

'Something like that.'

'Where are your garden gnomes?' she asked finally.

He said no more, not looking either at her or his picture.

'Is that all?'

'One more.'

She signalled him, a brief push with her forefinger, to turn on.

Again the same patch of English garden, the lawn shaved in stripes perhaps only minutes before the events depicted, the fence behind freshly painted, the rose bushes, the dwarf brooms, a magnolia spring-new and neat, though above, the sky was blotted black, wildly dark, threatening from the opaque complexity of black in the centre to a raggedness of darkling purple on the fighting edges. This time no firing squad occupied the foreground, but on the bourgeois tidiness of the grass a rifle had been dropped, abandoned; it gave the impression of crookedness, of a twisted and rusty anger combined with paradoxical murderous efficiency. At the far end this time were three bodies, not one, and though they had been obviously shot, all three were blackened with gushed blood on the chest, their arms were stretched out on cross-pieces and the middle corpse, slightly larger, wore a disfiguring head-piece, a hessian roll or a crown of thorns. The three bodies were hardly human, having collapsed, mere creased convicts' suits, ugly bundles held up by the wrists roped to the crossbars, heads sagging as if the force of the bullets had gouged out, flung away the offal of their trunks.

Ursula said nothing.

Worth opened a sketchbook where crooked hands, badly combed hair, pin-toed, booted feet were tried out, twisted and repeated, again, over and over, not for practice, it seemed, but out of obsession, and a pain of repetition.

He opened the book carelessly, flicking over the pages with

little reference to her while she squinted away. Perhaps a third of the way through, he suddenly, without a sound, closed the volume, pushing it off, and stood leaning hard, both arms stiff, on the end of the table.

She reached out, dragged the book rudely towards her; on the covers he had written in black felt-tip in Greek, ΤΕΤΕ̄ΛΕΌΤΟΧL, sprawlingly.

'What does that mean?' she asked.

' "It is finished",' he answered, throat clogged with phlegm. 'Uhh.'

They stood then, she with one corner of the sketchbook lifted from the table, he bent, neither speaking, each unable to look at the other. At the end of three length-dragging minutes she said brusquely, 'Put them away.'

'Uuuh?'

She signalled her command this time with her right hand. As he straightened himself he groaned, weakly, not noticing the sound, but closed the covers and replaced the sketches and the book quickly, unobtrusively.

'Shall we go out?' he asked, fastening the cupboard doors. He waited for her to lead the way, did not touch her. In the hall she hesitated. 'Kitchen,' he ordered, but gently. 'It's warm there.'

They sat down, on the red-topped stools.

'What do you think?' he asked.

'Will the Arab be interested? In a Crucifixion?'

'No. Did you like them?'

'It wasn't you, somehow. It was as if you were out looking for trouble.'

'Isn't that what Walden wanted?'

'Perhaps.'

'I did the last one in a great hurry, when I thought I'd finished. I was walking along a street and there was a rotten printed notice for Good Friday services and at the top this Crucifixion scene with dashes suggesting light. A black and white affair. And I thought, I'll make my execution squad shoot Jesus and the thieves. I did a few sketches on my block and worked at it straightaway, next morning. I kept Sibelius's Fourth blaring away on the stereo. And when I'd done it, I told

57

myself, That's that series finished.' Worth writhed as he sat.

'And was it?'

He didn't answer immediately, coughed, stumbled to his feet and out. He returned carrying a small canvas, just under a foot square.

'It's not dry yet,' he whispered.

She saw it from a distance, a head, the head of the executed man, or mostly from its position, the hair, the short, luxuriant, rough-combed locks, dragged away from the parting. He handed it over. The painting was strikingly achieved, the hair in thick, daubed links so that its brown brightness and dullnesses seemed to squirm pressurized, not like live snakes but with the thick torpor of heated glue, ready to burst into bubbles, to sear and blister a probing finger. Little of the face could be seen, but she could make out from that little that the painter had limned himself.

'It's you,' she said.

'Not the mop, though.' He seemed almost cheerful.

'You as dead Jesus.'

Ursula moved it here and there in front of her face; she saw no more in it wherever she held it; she hated it everywhere.

'It's rubbish,' she said.

'No,' he answered, 'it isn't. I may not have got it right, but I'm trying to say something.'

'Such as what?'

'That nature's as beautiful, and men as careful of their gardens even when horrible massacres happen in them. Perhaps that's what keeps us sane.'

'Painting yourself dead, shot? Keeps you sane?'

'You wanted a dead body under cherry blossom. You got it. Now you don't like it.'

'I loathe it,' she said, near shouting, unusually for her.

'I told you all along that there was plenty to occupy my technique with horse chestnuts and dead elms, but you wouldn't have it, that there's plenty to fire the widest-ranging imagination in the dullest back street in this town, but oh, no. You must have your corpses and your public executions. There they are. And you don't like them.'

58

'Neither will Walden,' she said caustically.

'Probably not.' He mumbled, losing heart, as she put down the oil sketch and filled the kettle.

'So what will you do next?' she asked brightly from the sink.

'Pear blossom. Women's bums.' He had recovered, had picked up his picture, was carrying it away grinning. They did not speak again until she had poured coffee; he stood all the time she was on her feet.

'Drinking coffee doesn't alter anything,' she said. 'Besides, you didn't even wash the mugs. How do I know this is mine?'

'Are you frightened you'll catch something?'

She didn't answer. He hovered about, not sitting, wanting to please.

'Will you send them to London?'

'Might as well.'

'Even though he won't touch them? I don't like those first two, either, those with no people in them. They're badly wrong, somewhere.'

'How do you mean? Because of the later . . . ?'

'No. They're crude, in some way. Blown-up photographs would have been preferable.'

'Yes,' he answered. 'Not bad, not bad. That's right. I painted them and thought about what I was going to do, and it roughened me up. They're unfinished, mere slapdash, by my standards, because I was painting into grass and trees what I was to do next, rifles and bullets and dead men.'

'But aren't the lawn and the garden better-handled in the last two?'

'Possibly; they represent only themselves, not cruelty or anger or judicial murder.'

'I wouldn't have guessed,' she said, 'from the first two that you wanted me to think about those horrible things.'

'What would you have thought then?'

'That you hadn't bothered or were trying out some new style you weren't familiar with.'

'I was.'

She looked poised, Sunday-beautiful there, one shapely leg crossed over the other, her face untroubled, the blue eyes wide and complacent. He seemed withdrawn, disappointed, angrily silent.

'An inconclusive evening, really,' he said, at length.

'I don't know what to say.'

He took her in his arms, kissing her fiercely.

'No, she said. 'Not that.'

'Not that,' he mocked.

'No,' she said, pushing. When she had backed off she spoke, low but fiercely. 'You can't cure everything with a bear-hug and a kiss.'

'I can try.'

'You can't. And I'll tell you why: because I shan't let you. I've looked at those sketches of yours tonight, and I feel degraded. You've prostituted yourself.'

'Look, you're not very logical. You wanted Walden down; you came in to cook lunch so he could spend all his time instructing me. When I follow . . . '

'There's something wrong with those sketches as sketches.'

'What?'

'I don't know. I can't explain. You wouldn't understand. It's not only that they've got no social significance. It's as if you'd been so concentrated on the horror that you'd forgotten how to draw and put paint on.'

'That's rubbish. I tried to suit my technique to my subject matter. The fact that you don't approve of that subject matter is what's put your back up. I was frightened of what I was doing, but determined to come up with something. I don't know whether I've got it right. Being a pessimist I suspect I haven't. But I sweated blood, and when you mince round with your prejudice and airs and graces, I think to myself, she's supposed to be on my side; and I give in.'

'I'm sorry.'

'You're not. You're pleased to see me down and out. You spit on the corpse with pleasure.'

'I'd better go.'

He did nothing to prevent her. She wished him goodbye politely enough, closed his door quietly while he returned to two unoccupied stools, two mugs of coffee, hers barely half-drunk.

60

8

Worth wrote to Walden explaining what he had done and why he found it unsatisfactory and receiving no reply took himself off to the Peak District to sketch. There he concentrated on streams, on brown fast water frothing over stones. Though the weather was bleak, so that his fingers froze round his pencil, the play of bursts of sunlight excited him, and the sharp bouts of exercise kept him cheerful. He had left no messages behind, but began to long for home after three days; holidays were good, times for preparation, but the need for his studio, his work soon made him uncomfortable. On the fourth day he was caught in a snowstorm, more boisterous and lengthy than he had expected, so that by the time he'd struggled down to the farm at the head of the village the ground was covered white-over.

A farmer, in flat cap and waterproofs, blundered across the road.

'How long's this going to last?' Worth shouted.

'Urggh.' The man pulled his cap down, looked him over, eyebrows beetling. His dog circled.

'Unseasonable for April?'

'Not up here, it i'n't.' He turned, intent, his face grim.

Soon the weather cleared, but Worth had had enough, packed his traps, sat warm behind bus windows until he landed home to prepare in time for his stint on Miriam and Victor. Grateful for the occupation, he found himself fluent, completing a month's graft inside a few hours. Always suspicious of too easy a progress, he put the day's tally aside in the expectation that next morning he would discover its worthlessness, and made out for the streets. He chased after half an hour's fast walking, towards higher ground where a huge estate of private housing had been perched up and down the low hills.

He rarely came this way as the place depressed him. He

remembered that twenty-odd years ago his father had brought him out here on Sunday afternoons, and then it had been farmland, crossed by a sandy rutted lane between hawthorn hedges, odd country, different, both rural and dirty. Once one had climbed for a few minutes one could see out to the town but that had appeared distant and itself surrounded by fields. The factory chimneys, the terraced streets, the chapels, pubs, the humdrum church on its pimple of a hill had been misted, lost sharpness whatever the weather, become a holy city, invested with a grey glamour unconnected with manufacture, paving stones, unemployment, petrol fumes, families, money.

Even at that time, the first signs of change were evident, surveyors' pegs, the abandonment and vandalism of farm cottages and finally the demolition of a narrow, disused railway bridge and the mechanical digging of a vast sewer. Now the mildly rising hills were covered with open-plan streets, neat detached houses with garage and a Ford or polished Vauxhall, Datsun, Toyota, in the drive, small terraces of jagged maisonettes, with here and there a bungalow, and finally a half-built shopping precinct marooned by a useless stretch of tractor-rutted mud. These hillocks formed a perfect setting for town dwelling, but the houses seemed to straggle, uniform and shoddy, small private boxes of rubbish, painted with care to clash with the neighbour's handiwork, the small squares of lawn cut trim, the windows widely bare or frilled with pastel lace, the shrill shouts of children everywhere. Decent people lived here, Worth told himself, lived comfortably, but he could not believe it. Someone fried onions until the sloping street reeked.

He walked on, and surprised himself by discovering near the shops somewhere towards the middle of this huge sprawl of new brick and mortar a hundred yards of hawthorn hedge with its accompanying dirt path. He remembered it clearly; to the other side had stood a farm, in the dale, its yards crowded with rusty harrows, old tyres, a tractor, a lorry, wooden carts, and long puddles almost as dark as the surrounding mud. At the end of the surviving hedge, he recalled, the footpath had dipped. He strode out to try the land again. It fell sharply, unmodified by excavators, but ended in a small playground, a roundabout, a slide, a swing, all set into tarmacadam. The few playing urchins glanced briefly up at him before continuing their half-hearted pursuit of mobile pleasure. As a boy, not much older than these, he'd stood on much the same spot on a day in winter. He'd been invited, if his memory played no tricks, that night to a Christmas party, a rarity.

Then he had been walking with schoolfriends, and his anticipation of the evening's entertainment had been bright enough to shift the coldness of the afternoon, and yet now Worth remembered nothing of the event itself. It had faded so that only his delighted desire for it remained, like this hedge, petering out, a small useless monument, displaced, of no value, demonstrating if anything the inefficiency of planners who hadn't the necessary technique to incorporate the rural strip into the grand design or the lack of it. He closed his eyes, opened them to gloom down on the children he did not see.

He strode away, in the maze of houses, the closes and crescents, once crossing a wide highway by an underground tunnel, the concrete walls sprayed with a dullness of graffiti: Forest = magic; Skins Rule OK?; The King is Dead; Hang all Wogs; Led Zeppelin. As he walked slightly uphill, enjoying the exercise, he heard, with unbelief, the skirl of bagpipes and stopped. He could not doubt, and as he quickened his pace, the sound blared larger. He turned a corner, and there, by a small detached house, one of six, a young man marched up and down the flagstones of his garden path. The player walked smartly, turned about, made for the front gate, back again, the sound of his pipes reedily echoing from adjacent walls. Worth stood, hoping the man would speak, but he continued the quick traipse and wheel, scattering the sour sounds with a smart virulence of effort. A man in a charcoal-grey suit, with a cream shirt and maroon tie, jacket flapping, he concentrated on his self-imposed task. No one else looked out; evening sunshine cast long shadows; cars stood ready for the jaunt or next day's sweat, but this individual, dark hair bouncing, horn-rimmed glasses slightly askew on the round, red face, forced his practice on the street undeterred. Worth had no idea whether he played well for he disliked the bagpipes, except on ceremonial occasions, with footguards and floodlights. 'Pibroch of Donuil Dhu, Pibroch of Donuil,' he quoted, and turned aside, dissatisfied, again with a raw image of his own proceedings. Here a man practised an art for which there could be little call, and perhaps turned out by his wife risked mockery in the streets without reason, but he played and swaggered.

Worth felt cheered and dashed at this example of the unwanted. No sooner was he out of earshot of the pipes than he checked at the sound of the piano from a bijou home, Tudor beams bright blue, pebbledash yellow as scrambled egg. He almost recognized the air, played with a stumbling élan, and edged closer to listen, his eyes fastened onto a small silver birch in the front garden. 'Für Elise'; he used to hack through it himself, Beethoven's album-leaf. Only that week he'd heard some know-all on the radio pronounce the title due to the composer's bad handwriting; he'd really intended Thérèse. There were no mistakes about the music; it moved with limpidity, simple and lucid, attractive, able to withstand a hundred repetitions, scores of amateur wrong notes. Who played the piece he did not know; he attributed the sounds to a girl, he could not say why, but for all he knew it may have been the mother, proud of her new house, determined to use the piano now she had room for it. A man weeded his garden nearby, unheeding, motor-mower at the ready. A tame cock blackbird lifted a beak stupidly at the alert. This street seemed placid, untroubled by motorists, peaceable except for the soothing rise and fall of the piano and yet, it was possible he'd only to turn the corner to run into a street game, a concrete-mixer, some ground-shaking pop from forty-watt speakers.

After a further ten minutes he made his way back, uncertain, unwilling to trust the proliferation of roads, their exaggerated, neat boredom. He came downhill almost at the run, into the yellow brightness of the western sky. The pace exhilarated, as his feet slapped pavements, but he felt out of place, in a wilderness, lost, deserted by these good people who lived here with their f.g.c.h. and new stair carpets. At the bottom of the hill, on the main road, he reached the pub, modern, pushy, four-square, lights on already, the Huntsman. He had bet himself on the colour of carpets, and walls, the choice of bar furniture and mirrors, the landlord's blazer buttons, before he decided against patronizing the place. He joined, crossed the A-road beyond the site of the old bridge and there watched the constant stream of cars, smoothly accelerating, sweeping towards an evening's pleasure. He swore, but his annoyance was directed against himself rather than against the homes and transport of his fellow men. As likely as not they were as dissatisfied as he.

He crossed the common by a footpath, braving the late golfers.

Back amongst the semidetached and then the terraced houses he became more at ease. Here the low sun darkened the clefts of the streets, and few people were about. Worth, walking fast, had decided on a course of action: he would go to visit Ursula. He usually telephoned, but tonight he would present himself at her door, without excuse, and she could make of it what she liked.

No one answered when he rang the doorbell. He pressed again. At the third summons Ursula appeared, head turbaned in a towel.

'I've just washed my hair. Come on upstairs.'

In her bedroom she unswathed her hair, set to work on it with comb and drier. The noise of the machine precluded chat.

'Well, what are you doing here?' she asked, switching off, but not facing him, concentrating on her reflection.

'I wanted somebody to talk to.'

'About what?'

'That's it, really. I don't know.' She worked on with her comb, too occupied to answer. 'It needn't be about anything, need it?'

'You tell me,' she said unsympathetically. A minute or two later when she had relented sufficiently to ask about his Derbyshire jaunt, he answered, as if he had to win her favour. She heard him out, unimpressed, and inquired about Walden.

'Nothing,' he said. 'Not a word.'

'Has he seen your Crucifixion pictures?'

'No. I explained about them, but didn't send them.'

'Why not?'

'He wouldn't touch them.'

The comb in her right hand mastered her wet hair as her fingers moulded. She made, unmade, reshaped as if it were an exercise, or for exercise. He admired the muscular energy of her arms, the precision work, the movements rapidly executed, erased, repeated; her brush added to the controlled violence.

'How do you know that?' she asked.

'You said so yourself.'

'That's nothing to go on.' She sounded exactly, hatefully, like her father. 'When you start quoting me, you must be short of something to say.'

'Probably.' Sulking.

'And what do you intend to do then? Go back to your trees?'

'Very likely.'

'That wouldn't be a bad thing,' she said, 'especially if you've learnt something. Have you?' Immediately she snapped on the whining drier to scour off his answer. He waited as she, utterly intent on her hair, bent forward to fluff and place and play.

'Well?' She had finished now, or paused.

'I don't know,' he said. 'How the hell should I?'

'Try something else, then. Some new technique, if you won't alter your subject matter.'

'Painting with my eyes shut?' Sarcastic.

'I won't say you do that already, but you're next door to it. You've had two or three shots at executions, and then you're on to crucifixions, but you don't care who's been shot, and for what reason. You're horrifying us, that's all. Why don't you go down to the hospital mortuary and paint smashed up corpses, or postmortems?'

'That's not sensible.'

'This man, Walden,' she said, rounding on him with the comb, 'came up here to force you to feel and see differently. But what do you do? You act like somebody trying to swim at the same time as keeping both feet on the bottom of the bath. And the result? It looks bloody ridiculous, and moreover you'll probably drown yourself.'

'That's what you think?'

'You don't want to change. It's not that you can't paint. Your technique's adequate. You're a magnificent draughtsman, one of the best in England. Look at those hands you drew. But you don't want to feel. You're not interested in human beings. Drawing men as lumps of meat doesn't mean you've . . . ' She broke off, not bothering now to fiddle with her hair.

'What's got at you?'

'You ask for advice,' she snapped, 'and when it comes you don't like it.' She swung round again, frowning as far as she could, flushed, in ache. 'Why did they shoot those men? You hadn't considered it. You don't know if they're communists or fascists, and you don't care, either.'

'Would that make a difference?'

'You wouldn't ask that question if you didn't know the answer.'

'It may surprise you, but I don't think that it would have made a ha'porth of difference.'

'That's what I'm telling you.'

'I don't understand you.'

'Whose hurt hurts you? Come on, tell me that.'

'Famine. Those children in Somalia. The Vietnamese boats. Belfast and Newry. El Salvador.'

She waited before answering, expecting justification. Embarrassment darkened his face.

'I knew you could read the newspapers,' she said, in the end. 'But do these things alter your painting?'

'Yes.'

'I doubt it. You're a decent man, but you don't think your paint-on-paper will have the remotest effect on any of these. No. That's perhaps a proper modesty. But do these have any effect on you? That's what matters. Off you toddle to sketch your ash trees once again, as if everybody in the world was as comfortable as you. They're not.'

'What's wrong with you tonight?' he asked.

'Never you mind what the motive behind my criticism is. Is the stricture correct?'

'Stricture,' he said. 'My God.'

'This man, Walden, if he's genuine, came up here to try to harness your technique to some matter worthy of it. I admit doubts about that, to myself. Chiefly because he seems to be trying to wangle you a commission on the walls of an oil sheik, which, in my view, is not the place for serious or moral art. Perhaps it just provided a reasonable excuse to intrude into your affairs. I don't know. But it's time somebody did.'

'You sound just like your dad.'

'We're talking about you.'

'And you're quarrelling with me so that I'll paint better?'

'I'm stating the obvious,' she said. 'You have reserves of talent you never touch, and never will, if it's left to you.'

'I see.'

Both sat there, as if temporarily exhausted, weakened by truth and its ill-tempered approaches.

'Go on downstairs,' she said. 'And get me a glass of gin and ginger, and something for yourself. Go on. Skedaddle. I'll be with you in a minute. For God's sake. Don't stand there like a dying duck in a thunderstorm.' She tried roughly to be kind, he recognized.

When she arrived in the kitchen she looked too spruce, too well laundered; her perfume stung.

'Cheers,' she said, lifting her glass, sitting down with a fuss.

'That's better.' He swigged at his whisky. 'If I could get half seas over I'd perhaps paint what they want.'

'What would the subject matter be?' Coolly.

'Skinheads. With big boots.'

'Not a bad idea. Go and look and draw them.'

'I wasn't serious.'

'I am. The uneducated unemployed. The undeserving we don't want to know.'

'I'll tell you something,' Worth said. 'I don't understand you. I want somebody to hold my hand and flatter me, and all you do is sink your teeth in where it hurts most.'

'Good.'

'Good, my arse. I suspect I'm falling down on this commission, failing. I'm not up to the challenge. And I don't like it.'

'As long as you fight . . . '

'But what or who am I supposed to be fighting?'

'Yourself. Now drink your whisky and go off home.' She saw the disappointment in his face. 'I mean it.' She examined her fingernails. 'This is my evening for personal beautification, and I don't like it interrupted. I saw your friend Millicent Turnbull the other night.' Kindness again.

'Where?'

'At a meeting. I introduced myself.'

'What had she got to say?' he asked.

'Very little. She's not much of a talker. I told her my dad used to admire her husband.'

'Uh.' He finished his whisky. 'How did he come to be interested in rugby football?'

'I've no idea.'

'He never played, did he?'

'Not as far as I know.' Ursula stood, but walked, proud-backed, towards a mirror to re-examine her hair. 'She asked about your picture. Seemed really interested.'

'What did you say?'

'That you were pressing on with it.'

'And do you believe that?'

'Yes. Within reason. I hardly knew the girl, and so it seemed inappropriate to discuss your struggles and hang-ups. We didn't talk for long. She was shy, pleased somebody bothered to go over to her.'

'What was the meeting about?' he asked.

'Pollution. The environment. It would be, wouldn't it? All the bird-watchers and anti-vivisectionists. Interesting. It really was.' She laughed, and he was held at arm's length. 'I'm going to kick you out now. So, off you go and put your pencil to use.'

'What shall I draw?' he asked.

She considered, at uninterested length, and committed herself sarcastically. 'A religious picture.' Equally barbed; she was an atheist.

'With skinheads?' He matched her mouth; slouched off.

9

Worth left Ursula's door in a numbness of despair, but before he reached the end of the street he had thought how to occupy himself. The idea struck him as ludicrous, but he must try, and that as soon as he reached home. The madder the better. He took off his coat, warmed his hands, pinned a big sheet to his drawing-board and began. It was nearly nine o'clock.

'The Entry of Christ into Jerusalem.'

He sketched until the early hours, using notebooks, loose scraps for trial dabs, returning always impatiently to the large space. At one o'clock, he could hear it raining outside; he carefully replaced his pencils, squared up his bits and pieces and standing felt exhaustion. He directed his mind to comment on the composition, but he had no strength, no will. With an enervated pleasure his eye darted here, to this figure, to that doorway, spire, shadow. Shaking his head he covered the picture, not knowing why, perhaps so that in the morning he would have to make the effort to see it, not come on it unawares. The stairs stretched, treads high and awkward; once he stumbled, cursing.

In the morning he woke before seven, and disappointed by the postman and a late paperboy prepared and ate his breakfast before he mooched into the studio. Sun now shone mistily, but the radio forecast showers; he washed the dishes, banged about with the carpet-cleaner, wasted boring time on the newspaper, cut his fingernails, walked up and down the garden path, admiring lilac, aubretia, the velvet of wallflowers. In the end, knuckle-chewing, he unveiled the drawing.

Large, and violent.

Spaces were few and far between, for the crowds of figures seemed to be standing on a bank, or perhaps on garden walls, so that they reached up, spilled rather into the sky, while in the background the houses, the neat detached he'd observed yesterday though with roofs shimmering, seemed squat even though they were punctuated with frequent, unlikely towers and chapel spires. In the middle Jesus entered the Holy City on a motor-bike, standing on the pillion seat, skull shaved short, hands clenched above his head like a goal-scoring footballer, leather jacket open on naked torso, boots and leather trousers heavy, menacing, uncouth. His face, unbearded, grinned with a strength of teeth, in a grimace of unholy joy. The youth driving the bicycle sat upright, fáce straight as a court usher's or toast-master's knowing the value of ceremonial; dressed like his leader, he kept the machine steady in the narrow slit of road. Nearest the Lord jumped other young men and women, shingled, ripping down branches from the flowering cherry, the ornamental crab, to whirl aloft and dash wantonly fierce in front of the procession. But older people cheered, middle-aged men in collars and ties, women with shopping baskets, shrieking; children leaped; young and beautiful matrons pushed their prams out, salients of salvation, towards the advancing Messiah. Behind the bike a troupe of black-leather clowns whooped their dancing, unstable joy.

Worth looked on the picture coldly, aware not so much of the liveliness as of the many alterations he wanted.

He had no doubt he needed to try again. Quickly, unthinking, he opened a book, and began to make new outlines. Now the small cleared path turned so that it ran out on the bottom edge piled high with smashed branches, a denim jacket, a frock, a knitted football fan's striped bonnet, a scarf; this time birds watched as if there were silence and no movement, or as if they could be lifted down from the branches where they perched to lie brokenly happy in the road.

The phone rang.

Worth glanced at his watch; half-past ten. He had spent two hours at work, without noticing the chill of the room or his own desperation of effort.

'Hello.' He answered distractedly.

It was Millicent Turnbull.

'I'm glad I've found you,' she spoke breathlessly. 'I tried

71

twice last night, but there was nobody in.' He explained. 'It's Teddy,' she told him. 'He's ill.'

'What's wrong?'

'He was brought home from school, at the end of last week. He's had a breakdown.'

'Is he at home?'

'Yes. He's in bed now. Sedated.'

She, in small broken sentences, spoke of her husband's frustration, his blood pressure, his bursts of temper, his periods of silence and despair.

'I didn't like to say anything. To you, I mean. Or anybody else. It was like letting a secret out. He must have felt awful. But he just collapsed. He was gibbering and trembling. It was terrible to see him.'

'Did they take him to hospital?'

'No. They brought him home.'

'What's your doctor say?'

'He says he's been under strain. Now he's just to lie quiet.'

'Can he get up? Come downstairs?'

'If he wants.'

'Does he want to?'

'He's made an effort. Once or twice. But it's all physical, as if he's been beaten up.'

'Won't that be the drugs?'

'I don't know. Could be, I suppose.'

'Is he eating?'

'Not much. He's not very interested.'

Her voice was white, without harmonics, tissue-paper thin as if she could raise no more than a whisper.

'Are you there on your own?'

'Yes. The doctor comes in. He's been very good.'

'You can't go to work?'

'No. I'm taking some holiday they owe me.'

'Do Piers and Natalie know?'

'I wrote to Piers. Natalie's been to see him.'

'Would you like me to come round?'

'That's why I rang. He said he wanted to see you. The only one.'

72

'Don't the school . . . ?'

'They call,' she said. 'And he's had no end of cards. From the kids. It frightened them.'

'Are you coping?' he asked.

'I have to.'

He reached for his jacket.

On his way over, he decided what he would say to Millicent. She was to go out, the morning was bright, do her shopping, call in for a coffee at the Criterion or the Kardomah, visit a friend, treat herself to a change. Immediately he had shaken her hand, he issued these orders, but she shied uncomprehendingly from him, rushing, here to straighten a bibelot, needing to sit down and then immediately, nervously rise, fingers working.

She described, in between these flittings, how they had brought her husband blubbering home, a lump of weakness, crouping for breath, moaning, all without restraint, sobbing, as if he'd been monstrously struck down by some gigantic flu. Though her delivery was uneven, she had managed to stand back from this disaster, to describe it with a kind of naïve objectivity. She herself said that the whole thing was so unexpected and brutal that it removed her out of normality of response, made her a robot or nurse; it was only now that she began to feel it.

'How is he this morning?'

'Not too bad. He's had some tea and toast. And his capsules. He knows you're coming. I don't know whether or not he'll talk.'

'Does he tire easily?'

'Yes. He's sleepy. Dazed. That'll be the tablets.'

'Well, you write your shopping lists, and have a walk. The sun's warm out of the wind.'

'The neighbours are very good. I'll go and see if there's anything he wants.'

She remained upstairs, where there was some clumping about.

'He's ready for you,' she said.

'Does he want anything?'

'No. I took him to the loo, and then he demanded clean pyjamas in your honour.'

'He must be getting better.'

While she prepared her lists, collected bags, touched up her hair, Worth waited downstairs with her. She talked to him, smiling, moderately excited by her jaunt, slightly flustered by his observing presence.

'Up you go,' she ordered as she let herself out.

Turnbull sat in bed propped by pillows, the *Daily Telegraph*, still neat, in front of him, his reading glasses slipping low on his nose. He and his colleague shook hands self-consciously before Worth noticed that Millicent had placed a chair for him on the other side of the bed.

'Well, young man,' Worth said, moving round, 'and what have you been up to?'

'That's it,' Turnbull answered.

'You've been overdoing it, I hear.'

'Ah. That's about the length and breadth of it.'

Neither spoke easily; their sentences were pushed forward, like the preliminary moves of pieces in a game neither player was conversant with, where both expected some objection from the opponent or even correction by an umpire. Worth did not want to press his friend; Turnbull, ashamed perhaps, confessed only gruffly. They sparred, unaccustomed to boudoir speaking, for ten minutes, a quarter of an hour, both concentrating on the quilt during the awkward, clock-bothered silences.

'But you're improving?' Worth demanded.

'Isn't that how I look?'

Turnbull, in fact, did not appear ill; though he had lost something of his high colour, his hair was combed and he'd had a closer shave than usual. In pyjamas his shoulders seemed unusually broad, his wrists, hands and neck powerful, his head strongly set, his nose and mouth unsagging, almost young. His speech sounded slurred, but it took Worth some minutes to attribute this to the absence of a dental plate.

Put out by the sluggish conversation Worth described his sketches, his days in Derbyshire, his meetings with Ursula and ended, inartistically, hypocritically, with further, mostly fictional sentences, of praise for Turnbull, admiration, from Edgar Quinn. These were received without enthusiasm.

In return Turnbull complained about the school, the inefficiency of the headmaster, the lack of interest or professional skill among the teachers, the inattentive fecklessness of the bright, and the wooden stupidity, unchecked truancy, vandalism, disruptive insolence of the sizeable minority of delinquents who despised education as time wasted before the real life of unemployment and social security payments made men and women of them. Turnbull spoke without passion, was prepared to accept emendation or correction, even demonstrated his affection for his charges among the dull vagaries of personal pessimism, and apart from the slight impairment of speech it was little different from his usual description of his work and its frustrations. There'd be dozens if not hundreds of teachers in the town, Worth guessed, who would speak exactly thus, especially at the end of a long term or just before an examination. Bad enough, but nothing that a Friday night or a pint or two or a concert could not set to rights. Turnbull himself talked on as if he could hardly muster interest in what he was muttering, but needed obscurely to fill his leisure. Now and then he lost his drift and needed the listener to prompt him; illustrative anecdotes rambled shoddily dull as the argument.

'Don't tire yourself,' Worth advised.

'Tire? I'm glad to have somebody intelligent to talk to.'

'I'm sure Millicent comes up to scratch.'

'She's run off her legs, poor lass. And another thing is, I'd made up my mind not to burden her with my troubles. That was one of the snags with Elspeth. She'd complain from morning to night, if I'd let her.'

'Did you?'

'Eh?'

'Let her. Complain.'

'I'd no option.' He grunted, writhed. 'She sent me a get-well card.' He sat up to start and abandon a perfunctory search in a bedside cabinet. His rolling displaced the sheets, revealing he wore no pyjama trousers. 'I don't know where she's put the damned thing.'

'Is she still living hereabouts?'

75

'No. Leicester.'

'How would she know?'

'The children. Natalie, probably. She keeps in touch. I was surprised she . . .' He sat straighter. 'Will you get us a drink? I'm so dry, my mouth. It's these blasted tablets. There should be a bottle of lemon-barley somewhere.' Worth searched unsuccessfully. 'No? She's probably taken it away. She's a great shifter.' Another investigation failed to locate the drink.

'Where will it be? Downstairs?'

'Likely as not. On the kitchen table. Or in the larder. Big bottle. Grey stuff. You can't miss it. She probably took it down to wipe the bottom; it's sticky. Didn't bring it back. Go and have a look, would you? And bring a tumbler.'

It took Worth some little time to locate the bottle, and when he returned Turnbull did not drink eagerly, grimaced at the taste.

'Is it strong enough?'

'Muck. Can't fancy the stuff.' He blew his lips out. 'But she insists, and I humour her.' He put the glass down more than half full. Once again he began his tally of complaint about the school, listlessly retailing anecdotes of omission, malintention, commission, perversion; appearing himself invariably as a figure of common sense, who by some quick judgement or action or advice averted catastrophe; the place teetered on the verge of ruin or mayhem without him.

Worth listened glumly to the catalogue, because he remembered Turnbull as an outstanding teacher, firm in discipline, opening the eyes of his students to history, local geography, to civics. Five minutes of this whining voice would have goaded the most docile class to insurrection. Worth had always admired the way his friend ran over old blocks of fact as if they were newly minted, dropping his voice to a whisper at the very points about which he would later test the inattentive. Back rows had strained to listen to that still, insistent voice, and the big right hand, bunched or directing thirty-odd with one finger, demonstrated an easy mastery. Wrongdoers feared the broad, just shoulders, the bawled outbursts of feigned rage, the muttered audible insults; the unsmiling nod of approval, the congratulatory hand on a shoulder, the 'well done' sunnily but laconically delivered, earned rarely, wiped the air clear of thunder, made learning worthwhile. Beneath the skill lay a powerful belief in the validity of the exercise; it was to the advantage of these urchins to learn about their city and their country, about the law, the ideas and creeds, the historical events and figures, the castles and courts, the trades, the old stones and the new marble. They'd walk the street with their eyes wider, read their newspapers with understanding, teach their own broods, vote at every election because Old Bull had so instructed them. They'd forget much, some end up badly in prison, unemployment queue or bankruptcy court, but no one dared deny that what happened in Room 24 seemed important while it went on; old-fashioned it might be, based on the literary word, the archaeological logbook, the foundations of rationality and historical science, but it was delivered as if it mattered.

And now Turnbull lay here a nobody, a husk, a drool of a voice, a burden to himself, the family, the community.

The grousing dribble continued, with its sluggish tributaries of self-praise and reordered recollection. If there had been anything of interest in the room, Worth would have switched his attention, but the place was nondescript, bright, recently re-papered, with bed, dressing-table and wardrobe secondhand contemporary, veneered oak, factory-produced for the sunlit semi. Elspeth had decamped with the contents of the original best bedroom, and now Turnbull and Millicent had been round the sales of hire-purchase returns to cobble this clutter together. Who had made the choice? Surely the colonel's daughter had been used to something more substantial, more stylish than this? Turnbull, then? He'd no eye; Elspeth had bought, and removed, the Paul Nash, Matthew Smith, the Cézanne, the Corot, Pissarro and Sisley reproductions that had hung downstairs, and so, with money short, the adulterous couple, the newly-weds had invested their few pounds on this tat. Worth wondered what the drawing room would be like once Millicent had redecorated it. The listless voice was explaining that the headmaster had been warned countless

77

times, but had paid no heed, and that when the expected had happened had crept up to his depluty and shocked. What the disaster was Worth neither knew nor cared; it merely increased his unease. His mind drifted, and when it settled back some young four-eyed whipper-snapper who'd never been nearer a rugby pitch than his twenty-four-inch screen was being blamed for laying down the law about tactics, why Welsh backs or packs were invincible, to Turnbull who'd upended and scragged blues and internationals by the score. Nobody regarded experience; youngsters argued without respect, rushed past to their own trivial, haphazard devices, committed avoidable errors, would not admit blatant fault, then cried when they had been hurt.

'And so it all came to a head?'

Worth was not sure that he had actually interrupted, spoken the words out loud until Turnbull's eyes swivelled, bulged in his direction. Silence settled uncomfortably; the invalid rallied to think.

His account of the breakdown was short: he had slept badly for some weeks, but had felt no worse that morning than at other times; suddenly he'd lost control, in front of staff, pupils, dinner women, after the theft or misplacement of mathematical instruments needed for an examination. The groaning, the staggering collapse, the incoherence of tears had seemed not to be happening to him and even in his distress he found them incredible, unlikely, uncharacteristic. The physical body had lurched beyond control, but his eyes noted the frightened faces, his limbs had revealed to him what it was like to be laid along four staff-room chairs, while the headmaster stood by to attention, and some busybody rang the doctor's surgery and the young wife for instruction. Turnbull observed, in the disintegration of his persona, in the feverish dissipation of his moral fibre, what was happening. He could not prevent it; he shamed himself but it was as inevitable as the effect of gravity in the universe.

'They brought you home?'

'In the end. There was talk about ambulance and hospital, but they drove me back in my own car.'

'And stayed with you?'

'Until Milly came, yes.'

'Were you better? Once you were out of it? At home?'

Turnbull shook his head grimly; nothing so easy. Awkward silence again.

'The doctor came round?'

'First call. I'd got up to bed. He gave me an injection.'

'I see.'

The sick man lifted his head in dull surprise at Worth's answer. He sighed windily.

'Does he say how long it'll be before you're back to work?'

'The quack? He's given me a certificate for another month.'

Worth, reflecting, found he had little notion of the words Turnbull had used to describe his breakdown, and yet he felt its strong pain so powerfully that he wanted to crouch on his chair, stock still, to preclude further revelation. Speech seemed now near-blasphemy. At the obscene shattering of this good man, he wished to back away, to pass on the other side, to fail to think, to euphemize with unmoving lips.

Turnbull, though now more slowly, mulled over his grievances while Worth wondered whether his friend would recover. In the end he bluntly asked, and again Turnbull stared, cleared his throat, demanded, but took before he could be given, the glass of lemon-barley. He wetted his lips, ponderously, as if delaying the answer.

'They say so.' 'The quack' had grown into the wider pronoun.

For how long? When the poor man had been put back on his feet, would he be again reduced in a few weeks or months to his incapacity, or would the break have strengthened him sufficiently to see his time out?

'I had a car,' Turnbull said. 'An old A40. Fifth-hand to start with, and it creaked and groaned, always in at the garage. Then Elspeth hit a concrete lamp standard, not travelling fast in a fog, but I thought it was a write-off. Walter Weightman at Bexon's took it in, patched it up, cost me a hundred and thirty pounds, lot of money at the time, but I never had any more trouble. Had it for another three years; went like a bird.'

The parable.

'That's you, is it?' Worth asked, laughing.

'There's somebody at the back door,' Turnbull said, off-hand. 'Go down and see who it is.' His voice, phlegmily disturbed, lacked the energy of impoliteness. Worth, glad to leave, found Millicent clearing a trolley and a shopping-bag of groceries.

'You've been quick.'

'I don't like to leave him too long.'

'Don't trust me, eh?'

'It's not you. I'll make some coffee.'

She smiled, but he guessed her weariness at the querulously grumbling patient upstairs.

'Shall I go back?' he asked.

'No. Sit down here until I've put this lot away. Then I'll boil the kettle.' She rushed about efficiently, humming to herself, smiling each time her eye caught his so that he realized she enjoyed his company, his presence, even though they exchanged no words. When she had completed the chore, removed the receptacles, she darted for the kitchen and returning said, 'I'll just go up to milord. Turn the kettle off when it whistles.'

Once more he heard the thumping about upstairs, the duet of voices, the soprano the more volatile, dominant, though Worth could not make out a word. She came down, asked him to take the biscuit-barrel up.

'Leave it there,' she ordered, 'and come back.'

'We're not having our elevenses with him?'

'No.'

She had made the coffee and was sitting primly at the table when he returned.

'I can't get him to wear pyjama trousers,' she began. 'I tell him he looks disgusting.' She giggled. 'He says, "There's nobody to look at it but you, and you've seen it plenty of times." I can't understand him.' Worth thought of the broad, hairy arse turning in bed. She blushed.

'Is he a good patient?'

'Yes and no. He grumbles. He's impatient. But he's been sleeping a lot. I suppose that's the drugs.'

'Will he be able to go back to school?' Worth asked.

'Oh, yes.' Certainty rang in the voice. 'This may be a blessing in disguise. I thought he'd have a stroke or a coronary thrombosis. But he's up there, quiet, losing weight.'

'I thought the tablets made you gain . . .'

'Not these.' She offered him a newly opened packet of chocolate digestives. She laughed again, without hysteria but strongly. 'He's allowed two water biscuits. He might not want them.' As she talked on, Worth felt his confidence grow because she commanded the situation. 'I shall go back to work next week, and he'll be able to manage. We'll eat our main meal at night. We did before. He was dieting because school dinners are such stodge.'

'You'll be able to leave him?'

'I'll get Vera, next door, to come in. Then he'll have to put his pyjamas on. She's an old maid.'

Millicent talked easily, cheerfully now, and began to tell him how she had met Ursula Quinn, at a meeting about pollution.

'Did she tell you she'd seen me?' she asked him.

'Yes. She did in fact mention that you'd met.'

'Didn't she try to make you go with her?' Millicent pressed again genially.

'No, she has more sense.'

'Would it be wasting her time?'

'Why should it?'

'I don't know. I thought she'd want to convert you.' Millicent cocked her head to one side. 'She's very left-wing, isn't she?'

'Radical. Uuh. Yeh.'

'She was with a little group who gave the chairman a tottering time. A young chap with a mass of fair wavy hair, and a beard. He looked like a picture of Jesus.'

'Stu Stout.'

'Is that who he is?' Millicent seemed delighted. 'I've heard his name. He's always writing letters to the papers. Has she known him for a long time?'

'They teach at the same school, Welbeck Secondary.'

'They really badgered the chairman.'

'Sensibly?'

'Eh?' She was caught out, taken aback.

'Did they go for him because he was an obstructionist, or a fuddy-duddy, or a stuffed shirt? Or were you on his side?'

'I don't know, really. It was very exciting. People lost their tempers and heckled and shouted and made points of order.'

'And what did Ursula do in the war?'

'She sat in the middle of the group, and laughed a lot and clapped.'

'But didn't argue?'

'Not really. Not out loud. She prompted the others, I think.'

He brushed the crumbs from his pullover down to the tablecloth. 'And did you approve?'

'It didn't seem to matter. You know, I thought about it afterwards, and there didn't seem much difference between what the chairman wanted, and what they were shouting for. But they wouldn't let him soft-soap anybody. It had to be fierce.'

'Who was the chairman?'

'A Labour councillor. John Papworth, I think his name was. The bearded man kept calling him "comrade".'

'Yes.'

'What do you mean, "yes"?' she asked.

'Nothing. Nothing. I know him a bit, but I've no interest in local politics.'

'And she doesn't try to force you?'

'I wouldn't say that. She thinks I'm a bad case. I tell her until they vote to stop me using brushes and paints, they can get on and do as they like.'

'Isn't she angry with you?'

'Sometimes. Yes, she is. Now and again. But I think like you. They're all Marxists or Trotskyites because they must have some excitement to colour their lives. They'd hate to be told that. They think they're convinced by argument and intellectual rigour, the dialectic, and what-not, but . . .' He shrugged, swigged his coffee, said he'd his living to earn, spent a further five minutes upstairs in the company of man and wife, and went down to his studio, pleased with himself, as one justified.

10

He invited Ursula round to view his picture.

When the cloth was removed, she stared solemnly, then scrabbled in her handbag for a pair of tortoiseshell-rimmed glasses with huge, round frames before she scrutinized the paper comically.

'Go on,' she said, still intent. 'Tell me about it.'

'Christ's entry into Jerusalem.'

She was now bending, her face within a few inches of the drawing board, the spectacles snatched off and brandished.

'Is that all?' she said. He did not answer, and she whirled about, took a step or two away, paused, homed back fierce-faced. She stood, having boxed and put away her glasses, tapping her handbag, clicking its fastener. He waited.

'I don't understand you,' she pronounced. 'Why is Christ a skinhead?'

'You told me to.'

She registered bored impatience.

'Christ was a religious teacher. You may not approve of his line; you may think he was mistaken about being the son of God. But he was a moralist, a thinker, a thirty-year-old, not an adolescent ton-up kid.'

'I'm trying to suggest that's how he'd seem to the scribes and Pharisees, the establishment.'

'Why?'

'What do you mean, why?'

'If you'd made him a communist agitator, a dissident philosopher, even a mad scientist, I could have understood that. They are all unpopular, but they're all capable of consecutive thought and argument, however unacceptable. But what's your Jesus? What can he do? Stand on the pillion of a motor-bike and flash his fists about? What sort of teaching does that represent?'

'Don't you see that to his opponents he'd be as uncouth, and incomprehensible as this boy is to you?'

'It's like your executions. You're trying to shock, to act a bogey-man. You've no idea who's been shot, or why. And now here's your Jesus, uneducated, rough, a brainless yob. I've no time for Jesus. He was too concerned with religion, the kingdom of heaven, his Father's business and the rest of it, holiness, to have much relevance to our sort of world. But at least he was a thinker, an intellectual, astute at arguing his case against the doctors of the law.'

'I've shocked you, then, have I?' he asked.

'You wouldn't shock an old maid's budgerigar off its perch. There's no weight of belief there, no conviction, no real content. If you called it "Our Trev's Entry into Carrington Marketplace", I could have understood you, even appreciated the force of "entry". But Christ. Christ.'

'Is it the blasphemy?'

'Blasphemy's nothing to me. I don't understand it. Anything and everything should be criticized, even libelled.'

'Misrepresented?' he gibed.

She laughed.

'It's you. You don't care.'

'Basically?' he mocked.

'That's well drawn, lively. It's a bit like Stanley Spencer, full of energy. But you don't mean anything by it.'

'What can a picture mean? What do you want? Socialist realism? "Our Trev Leads the Workers' Rising"?'

'No, I want you to believe something so strongly that it strengthens your art.'

'My beliefs are aesthetic.'

'So if I asked you,' she said, 'to draw a daisy standing in water in an egg-cup, you'd make great art of it?'

'There's no reason why that shouldn't be the subject of a masterpiece. It doesn't suit me. I go in for the complicated, the highly intricate. I guess that the greatest works of art are the most complex. But that's me.'

'The sophisticate?'

He did not answer her, but re-covered the sketch.

'Don't do that,' she called sharply.

'You've seen. You've said your piece. I've listened.'

'I want to look again.'

He jerked back the cloth, which he draped over his right arm, and then stood to the side of the easel. She did not stir, stared, her lips slightly parted, slightly trembling, paler than usual. When she moved it was to ease a wisp of hair from her high brow, to glance away.

'Enough?' he asked.

She said nothing, but turned to one side, and he replaced the cover with an air of formality, making uselessly sure that the surface was smooth. Now they were quiet, neither looking at the other, both troubled by the physical acknowledgement of a rift which seemed to have nothing to do with art or politics, to exist in some incompatibility neither understood or could account for.

'Justify yourself,' she ordered. She signalled him again to remove the cloth; he obeyed, ironically bowing.

'The only way I can do that is with my brush and my pencil.' He spoke unemphatically. 'If I make the point that this Christ is uncouthly opposing the law, that's only a minor matter in my eyes compared with the lines, the strokes, the colour masses. I know you won't understand that. You sit and theorize with your Stuart Stout and his like about politics, but you'll never approach art.'

'We want to change the nature of society.'

'And I want to enrich it.'

'You work for an élitist few. What difference does it make to the unemployed that your pictures are hanging on the walls of those rich enough to buy them?'

'Would it make any difference if they were on free exhibition at the Castle?'

'Not much,' she said.

'Once you've admitted that, you've let out what sort of system you want.'

'If you're short of money and food, and are likely to be kept so permanently by society, you won't go round admiring pictures. You pick up your gun or your grenade.'

85

He paused now, waiting for her, gnawing ruminatively at the hard skin of his index finger. When he spoke it was slowly, in a semi-whisper, his head averted. 'You don't believe half you say. It's me you're disappointed in.'

Her face set sullenly proud. 'I think politics, the changing of society to affect, to ameliorate the lives of the majority is the ultimate in human endeavour. After that, education, the arts, sports, parks, travel, yes. But until men and women are granted the dignity as of right to earn their living, to work, those are secondary.'

'Yes,' he said quietly.

'What do you mean, yes?' She had flushed unprettily.

'Nothing.'

'You're not a fool.' She spoke heatedly. 'Though I sometimes wonder.'

He allowed a few seconds of awkward, antagonistic silence and then replaced the cloth, without permission or hurry, twitching it creaseless. The back he presented to her seemed obstinate, not so much a denial as an assertion of his failure to believe with her. After a moment he walked over to the door, held it open. She did not shift, or move the hands clasped behind her; strain showed in her face, but he waited politely, looking down at his non-too-cleanly shoes.

Now she made for the door, brushed past him, touching him as if part on purpose, dismissing him, with the bone of her elbow.

'Can I offer you a cup of coffee?' he asked in the passageway.

'No, thank you.' Ursula's voice, normal, unpolemic.

'You might be thirsty before you've finished setting the world to rights.'

'Do you think so?'

He backed away from her towards his kitchen. 'Thanks, anyway, for coming,' he said.

She shook her head, as if she struggled to understand something, and as he watched her his eyes, hatefully to him, watered. He placed his back to the light, sorry for himself. He did not trust his voice, which might break, against his will. The spring sunshine brilliantly flooded the kitchen behind him, spread its blond, pleasurable wash up the sober pattern of the passage wallpaper, highlighted her cheekbones, haloing the rim of her arms and shoulders.

Now he determined not to speak, waiting for her.

'Right,' she said. 'I'm on my way.'

'Don't go.'

She raised her eyebrows, but stayed.

'You've nothing to say in my favour, have you?' he began.

'Nothing new, no.'

'It's not my painting you're rejecting. It's me.'

She made a gesture of half-assent, nodding, pursing her lips.

'Why don't you say so outright?'

'Say what?' she asked.

'That you don't want any more to do with me.'

'Look.' She sighed, deeply, woodenly. 'You ask me up here to criticize your picture. When I do you take it personally.'

'You'd sooner be talking politics with . . .' He broke off, not knowing how to name them.

'I would. Because what we discuss is important.'

'That little group of yours will never be anything except a faction. They can oppose, and that's about all they can do. They'll soon be opposing each other; they'll break into splinters. They'll never do anything, because they'll never be cohesive enough.'

'You could have said that about every great reforming movement in the first place.'

'And all the other nine hundred and ninety-nine which came to nothing and we've never heard of. Politics in this country, and this is why you don't like it, is largely compromise, the art of the possible, the search about for allies.'

'Unlike painting?'

'God knows there are enough compromises in art, and learning from others as well as making do with what we've got, but in the end it's one man to one canvas, and a result there to be judged. Not hot air about what's to be done. We leave that to critics and that's the difference between me and your radical friends. I turn out pictures. Poor, provincial, politically vacant they may be, but pictures. Not guff, blether, hot air, jargon. Pictures. You can't criticize the productions of your little Russian comrades, because they don't exist and aren't likely to.'

'That's silly,' she answered. 'You can argue over the logic, or the relation to fact. We do, all the time. You can guess what chance ideas have of being accepted by other politicians, or what their effect will be on other reformers' programmes. And we examine society. If we manage to change that, people will live better because we've done what we've done. Even if we fail, it's still worth the effort.'

'Failure's inbuilt,' he said.

'I don't believe it. I grant you we attract lunatics, hotheads, extremists. But they're a small minority. They're not impor- tant.' She took a step; it seemed significant. 'Look, John, you're an intelligent man. Why don't you come and sit in with us? You'll know then about the world.'

He barked sardonic laughter. 'You deal in theories,' he said. 'Sincere, perhaps in the first place, but half-baked.'

'You'd learn the problems, then.'

'I've as good an idea of them as you and your cronies.'

'But they're not at the forefront of your mind. They're not jangling your emotions and goading your conscience when you paint, because if they were you'd turn out something vastly different.'

'Theory again,' he said. 'I could be tormenting myself half-mad about refugees or child-beating or unemployment and still be painting calm seas and windless nights. You can't pick up a picture and deduce from it what the man was obsessed with, personal, political, social.'

'But there are great political painters, great religious painters . . .'

'They painted what paid the rent.' He looked ashamed.

'Join us, John. Put your skill at our disposal.'

'You're not interested,' he said. 'You think art's a minor luxury, dispensable.'

'I don't.'

The two words seemed wrung out of her, so that she stood

inhumanly, like a scarecrow, limbs wrenched awry, the sap of her life drained off, a stick-woman.

'Thanks,' he said, voice like a dry cough. 'I think you would employ me. But if I sat at your meetings, I'd be bored, or, worse, argumentative, and angry with myself because of, of the silliness of it all, so that I wouldn't wait to . . . I'd take to drink, not drawing.' He smiled at her, softening the language. 'I'd be a cynic in no time. I'd lose what feeble beliefs I have. Sit down, Ursie. Come on into the kitchen.'

'No. I ought to go.'

'Just a minute,' he begged. She followed him, perched herself on a stool while he stood, back to the bright width of the window. 'I'm shallow. Over a wide area of my life I'm nothing, nothing at all. Just here and there, at random, differing from day to day, real depths split, open up, apparently small, easily overlooked. I can't, don't choose where they are, nor can I offer an explanation. But they are depths. It's irrational. While I was doing the sketches for that ash tree you've got, I was riddled and shattered with emotion. It wasn't about ash trees, as far as I could tell; it wasn't about me; my relation to the universe might be a closer description. Or the other way about. But there's no doubt I was powerfully invested by an ineffable, violent emotion in the preliminary period. I can remember standing by a railway crossing in the sunshine, incapable of anything except a shudder, and that wasn't observable, I guess. But as soon as I set about the first picture, yours is the third, I was cool, settled. And yet that period of turmoil must have had its effect though I don't understand why.'

Ursula listened neatly, cowed by the confession perhaps or tired. She had heard this before, but though it seemed credible, she could not bring herself to believe it. In this way he deliberately excused feebleness.

'Make a cup of coffee,' she ordered. 'I want to ask you something.'

He moved gladly, humming, and beating time with a teaspoon.

'Ask,' he said confidentially, jovially, as he presented her with the drink.

'You won't like it.'

'Try me.' He lifted his own cup, beamed.

'It's about Monica,' she said.

He frowned; his face pinched thin round the lips.

'I told you you wouldn't like it.'

'What about her?'

Monica Pilgrim had committed suicide.

'Are you sure you don't mind?' she asked.

'Go on.' He looked away, had forgotten his coffee, perhaps her presence.

'What happened to her,' Ursula averred, 'was a tragedy.'

'Yes.' Both studied cups.

'Did it affect your painting?' She gestured back towards the studio.

He did not answer immediately, though he showed no distress.

'It stopped me from working. For long enough. Six months or more. But you mean, don't you, did it deepen my work?'

'That's right.'

'After she killed herself, I was teaching and in a mess anyway; I did nothing, and when I started again I did drawings of streets, opulent streets becoming seedy, with sawn-off iron railings and unpruned trees. They were almost architectural.'

'Why did you do that?'

'I don't know. One of my professors had been keen on it, and it gave me something to do, something I was capable of. There was the complication I enjoyed, and problems that weren't too difficult to solve. It was like knitting, I imagine. It kept my mind plausibly occupied.'

'When did your painting come to grips with, with what had happened?'

'I don't know whether it did.'

She pulled an uneasy face, so that he continued.

'This stuff about time the great healer is true. At least in some sense, and with most of us. I can remember setting my easel up in Burwell Park; quite early morning with nobody much about. And I'd actually begun, paper pinned up, idea conceived, hand actually working away, when I suddenly remembered that I'd been in this place with, with Monica. As far as I know it hadn't struck me before. I can't say why. Not consciously. But you realize that I think the subconscious is very important. Anyway, I remembered. We'd had a quarrel there, about whether we were to go to Alton Towers. Just trivial. She wanted to. I didn't. She had a car and liked to give me treats.'

'And?'

'We made it up. I gave in to her. I usually did. But as I sat there on my stool it all came back, and the fact that she was dead. It was worse because I wondered how I would have acted then if I'd known she'd kill herself not a year later. She was trying to cheer me, and I was playing awkward sods with her. I remembered the way she stood and how she had almost shouted at me, "Just make yourself say yes, will you?" It seemed so odd.'

'It must have been awful,' Ursula said.

'No. Bearable. I felt uncomfortable, out of sorts, but as I worked on, the feeling disappeared.'

'I meant her death.'

'It was inevitable. I wouldn't see it. She had tried before. It was her way of asking for help.'

'But she finally did it seriously.'

'Who's to know?' His speech remained soft, reasonable, crisp. 'She might have expected someone to rescue her that time, but it didn't happen. I found her. Her door wasn't locked. She was in bed.'

'Had she left you a note?'

He paused, disliking her curiosity, but continued.

'She always did. She was a great writer of messages. One to her parents, one to her sister, one to me. It must have taken her an hour at least just to write those. She sat at her desk, and made corrections, crossed things out, you know, altered, and then put them into envelopes, and then had the pills and the whisky.'

'What time of day was it?'

'Morning. They found her in the evening. She had paid the milkman not long before, quite cheerfully, hadn't stopped the delivery for the next day.'

91

'And nothing could have saved her?'

'When they found . . . ?'

'No. Ever.'

'It's possible. A different doctor, or approach. A chance meeting near the end. If the milkman had come in for a cup of tea, or made a pass at her. When I look back, she seems now to have been heading straight for it. Nothing I could do could alter it.'

'But you were close, weren't you?'

'Yes. Lovers.'

'But you didn't live together.'

'I didn't want that. Nor did she, I think.'

'You couldn't do anything about it? But you say the milkman could?'

'I was the shackle round her ankles.'

'How? What do you mean?'

'I couldn't give her what she wanted.'

'Sexually?'

'No. That was just about the best of it. She needed somebody to support her day and night. And to support her in exactly the way she wanted. I wasn't having it. I couldn't be at her beck and call . . .' His sentence crumbled away.

'Even though you loved her?'

'Love,' he said, without rancour towards her, drily, as if she had broached an unexpected but not very interesting idea. He sighed, clicked tongue on palate, spread his hands feebly.

'I mean . . .' she began.

'You mean,' he interrupted. '*You* mean.' Bitter now, but not angry. Sour-sick. That quieted her so that they stood silent, a nothingness between them.

Ursula, rousing herself, eyes heavy still, pricking, said, 'You don't mind my asking you this?'

'Eh?'

'You don't resent my questions?'

'Of course I bloody well resent them. I'm a human being. But,' he grudged this, 'I think I know what you're trying to do. And I think I know it's for my benefit. Or, at least, that's your intention. You're making me serious, aren't you? Because you can't imagine that making a simplified copy of what I see is anything but triviality. You want me to teach, but to teach politically. And so you're saying that important, crucial things happen to human beings, more important than trees and blades of grass growing in fields. Monica died. She killed herself. You can hardly guess what I felt about it, because I've forgotten a good half of it myself. Did I take the blame? I did. Was there anything I could have done? There always is. But I stood there like a spare prick at a wedding and painted my ash trees.'

'I'm sorry,' she said. 'I shouldn't have brought this up.'

'Yes, you should. Make the pot boil over.'

'Johnny.' She'd never called him that before, and it dumbed them both. They drank their coffee, thankfully, insofar as it occupied them. Constraint between them stood iron-strong, but friendly, an antagonism of good intentions.

'I shall have to be off now,' she announced.

'Very good.'

He made no attempt to detain her, even when she kissed him fully but coolly on the lips. They walked, he slightly behind, together along the passage and when he opened the front door the shrubs, the wall, the houses beyond, the sky dazzled with light, a pantomime transformation. Worth wanted to say so, but refrained. Ursula moved on, continued her road, through the bright frame of the door, into the sharpness of the day, not looking back, not saying a word. She glanced at him, smiled briefly, as she fastened the outer gate. He did not close the door at once, but rattled the loose-fitting knob. No words appeared to be played with; he knew his body which waited, a box of unhandled sensations.

11

For some weeks Worth worked, hesitantly, on the theme of Christ's Entry; he heard nothing from Walden of Burden

Brothers and the impoliteness jarred. When in the summer he read about and watched on television the outbreaks of riot violence he changed his line: now the skinheads smashed plate-glass windows, hurled petrol bombs, and the twin waddle of community bobbies became a line of plastic shields in the flaring darkness.

Ursula continued to visit him, but rather like a general practitioner or a friendly social worker, involved but at a distance, smiling as she had smiled at everybody else. Worth himself, busy and preoccupied, found himself able to put up with, even to play up to, this behaviour, and the new relationship seemed acceptable to both, as far as he could judge. Neither acted seriously towards the other.

Once a week he visited Theodore Turnbull and the pair walked together towards the local park, a place of shrubs and sooty flowers where children scraped off the surface of the grass with games of football and cricket, and adolescents writhed in the clutch of love. Turnbull had lost weight, his suit sagged, but his confidence revived, so that now he began to criticize himself.

'I don't know what I'm doing here,' he groused. 'I should be back at work. There's Mill off at eight-thirty every morning while I'm still in bed, and then I totter out like some superannuated . . .'

'Usher?'

'I'll bloody usher you. I feel guilty. I'm fifty years of age, not a hundred and fifty. I should be back.'

'You cook the meals and do the ironing, don't you?'

'What sort of life's that?'

'Ask the women. But it makes it all easier for Millicent, doesn't it?'

'And it makes it all harder for me to start again when start I do.'

'You don't think of retiring?'

'At fifty? From the one thing I can do nowadays.' He broke off. 'That's doubtful, isn't it?'

The pair strolled on in querulous companionship which Worth, for one, did not enjoy, but he knew his duty miserably.

One Sunday, early sky brilliant, he heard on the seven o'clock news bulletin that there had been riots in the city in the small hours. He rose immediately, listened to the local radio for details, cooked a large breakfast in excitement, bolted it and packed his sketching bag. By ten o'clock he had reached the scene.

He had not known what to expect.

First he could not see onlookers; people had not rushed from their beds as he had. The sunny air was undisturbed over a street which consisted on the one side of Victorian bow-windowed houses, semidetached but not large, crumbling if decent, doors and woodwork incongruously jazzed here and there in yellow, azure, daubed pillarbox red. The front of one house was overlaid with neat, thin stonework; another had a Regency door; a third sported mock-Tudor panes; the small front gardens were neglected with trampled earth, metal detritus, a brand-new motor-cycle. He could see no damage. The district had dumped its respectability of eighty years ago, but beautifully laundered West Indian children, fresh as flowers, hair in corkscrews, set out hand in hand for Sunday School. To the other side of the road sprawled concrete blocks of flats, square, square-windowed boxes, buff in shadow, the colouring hoarse as a sore trachea, but big with covered passageways, and the empty spaces grim, ugly yards of undecorated, mortared eyesore strewn with chip-papers and forks, broken glass, a dead starling.

Worth sketched, fast, into a hand-block, then more carefully into a larger sketchbook, annotating his drawings. A small group, coloured, white, Asian gathered to watch, to question.

'A' you from the council?'

'No, he's the Post.'

''S Good, i'n't it? He's pur our dog in.'

Higher up the street he found the three shops where damage had been done. The corner grocery had both windows broken, but was not yet boarded up. Next door, a television dealer's had been looted, while the third, selling millinery, baby clothes, was untouched, as if the mob had grotesquely respected women and children in its wildness. Smashed glass had been swept up, but small daggers of it glinted in the gutter. Already brown paper had been plastered over the broken windows of dwelling-houses, so that the place appeared nondescriptly run down, sleazy, not much worse than usual.

Worth applied his pencil, and the solitary policeman came across to view the process. A crowd gathered in no time, so that Worth grinned to himself. The artist, the private man who locked himself away in his studio to thrash out his pieces, was here circus-performing in the street. His skills were intact, he found, as the bystanders gave voice. The police officer, a bearded lad in his early twenties, unsmiling but in no way aggressive, kept the group at a small distance from the executant; they were allowed to approach, stare shortly, but not to question, to move on before they resumed their average of ebullience. The presence of the constable, it appeared, had established this norm of behaviour, this friendly, inquisitive, acceptable reaction to the unusual.

Soon Worth had done.

'There was a fire up Hyson Terrace, mate.' A youth in sweatshirt.

'Last night?'

'Yes. They was holling petrol bombs.'

Worth continued with his present task, a broken window, slivers still precariously attached to the frame, and at the open front door two Muslim girls, brilliant in yellow, in braided blue, silently observing the street, their head-cover held in a natural modesty across the face. Once when the children seemed on the point of withdrawal, the crowds shouted, friendly rough, for them to stand still 'till 'e's finished you'. The two blushed, giggled, murmured, but held their ground.

'Were there many rioters?' he asked the constable.

'No. Bit of an offshoot. How many?' he returned the question, voice small, strong accent.

'Thirty-forty.' A grey, balding West Indian.

'Three 'undred.' This suggestion, from a childish treble, was greeted with an uproar of derision.

'Thirty.' The constable.

'Were they locals?'

96

'No, they was not.' Many voices. Some slight argument, but for the sake of excitement rather than the establishment of truth. Worth had another shot at the head and shoulders of one of the Pakistani girls, and then equally rapidly at the kerbstone, the cobbled gutter, a star of shattered glass.

A small elderly woman came up to the artist, detaching herself from the crowd, planting herself obstinately.

'It was no worse than it is most Sat'days,' she declared. The crowd – it increased from minute to minute – stood silent now at the oracle. 'There's always trouble. They smash the garages and the lifts. They shit and piss on the steps. Bleddy 'ooligans.'

'Who?' he asked. He had now taken a large page and was dashing down, in the roughest shorthand of strokes, the whole curve of the street, the black gashes of the shop fronts, then the packed lines of window, door, entries of the terrace, regular, crowding one upon the other.

'Them,' she said. He did not understand, but flew at his sketch as if his life depended on it. 'Them as lives ovver there.' She pointed at the desert walls of the flats, unappeasingly buff, handsome as sackcloth. 'Youths.' She stood on tiptoe to look uncomprehendingly at his scrawl. 'Yo' ask anybody. Ask this bobby.'

Worth turned the page, dashed down chimneypots, television aerials against the blue sky, the puffs of cloud.

'That'll do now,' the policeman said. 'You've all had a good look. Get off home.'

A faint movement of acquiescence which the officer quickly transformed into dispersal answered him. This young man seemed much at ease. 'Go on, lad. Your mother wants you. Off.' He stroked his beard, said sharply to Worth, 'Are you nearly done, then?'

'Well, yes.'

'I shouldn't hang about once you've got what you want. They're a funny lot round here. Don't know what's coming next.'

'I'm tempting providence, you mean?' Worth laughed. 'Can I sketch you?'

'And what'll the inspector say about that?'

'You'll have to report my presence, will you?'

'You'll go down in the notebook.'

'My name's Worth.'

'You're not breaking any laws. But I was on here three nights ago when we got the big bust-up. We don't want to encourage any more of that, I'll tell you.'

'They reported this,' Worth wagged his finger about the street, 'on the national radio news this morning. How would that come about?'

'God knows. It was hardly anything. Mad bloody kids who'd had one or two.'

'Somebody thought fit to make a song and dance out of it.'

The policeman shrugged; his face had become unexpressive, as if it were difficult to live in and adapt to this circumstance.

'That'll do for the morning, then,' Worth said. He packed his satchel. 'Thanks very much.'

'Righto, sir.' The constable had already turned his back, was standing by the ruined window of the grocery stores, looking up the side street.

Worth had not walked forty yards away from the scene when he was stopped, this time by a broad-built, middle-aged man who had been waiting for him, who loomed out from an entry.

'You a journalist?' the man asked, in *basso profundo*.

'No.'

'Doing it out of curiosity?'

'You could say so.' They had fallen into step. The man wore a good suit, but no tie in his carelessly unbuttoned collar. Gold-buckled chaplis revealed white, woollen socks.

'Do you do much of it?'

'Sketching, not damage?' Worth pleased himself with that.

'Drawing. I mean, are you a weekend painter?'

'Professional.'

'Commercial, are you? Teacher?'

'Not really.'

'Have I seen any of your work?' The man was persistent, arrogant in this. What I don't know isn't knowledge. 'Do you exhibit?'

'My name's Worth.' A milk float chinked past; the driver raised a hand.

'John Worth?'

'Yes.'

That settled the matter one way or the other, so that they reached the corner where the street met a treed avenue without further questions. Worth turned left, was about to wish his companion good morning when the man said, 'I own a couple of your pictures.'

'Oh, yes.'

'Bought them locally. Very good. You're getting a bit pricey for me now.' The man's red face creased comically. 'Still, you've got to live.' That required no answering. 'Would you care for a cup of coffee?' He pointed across the road at a brick wall behind which small trees, overgrown high shrubs massed. 'That's my place.' Worth said nothing. 'Go on, give it a run. My name's Edwin Smith.' He took Worth's elbow to guide him towards a substantial, paint-blistered door in the wall. 'Hope to God I can get in here. Don't use it too often, but there we are.' Cemented into the top of the seven-foot-high brickwork were thick points of broken bottle glass. Smith had turned his key, but needed to put his shoulder to the gate to force it resistingly open. 'Ought to keep it oiled.'

Behind the closed gate the day became suddenly, darkly dark. A cracked cement path, weed-punctured, had been reduced by shrubs to a passage barely eighteen inches across. Rhododendrons, laurel, house-high lilacs, an unpruned clump of hawthorn, laburnum, limes, uncut privet clustered hostile, soot-dark, damp-smelling. The two pushed through, Smith first.

'No way to bring your friends,' he said, not displeased.

They emerged, turned right by the blank wall of the house and into the garden which bounced with light. A lawn, of public park proportions, was surrounded by thin beds of hybrid tea roses in bloom; the effect was, after the neglected murk of the shrubbery, one of intense brightness, the rose bushes stretched high, but also one of order, though imaginatively mediocre. One conjured up a small squad of men pruning and weeding thinking of knocking-off time, of catalogues consulted and nothing below the dozen bought, of large space filled, effectively but without care or affection.

'I'm no sort of gardener,' Edwin Smith said, 'but I do my best with some help.'

They proceeded by six steps to a terrace in front of the house, and a portico, the pillars freshly painted. In the hall, a blonde young woman wearing an open housecoat with a bikini beneath asked if it were warm enough to sit in the garden. Smith answered noncommittally, but made no introduction. The staircase splayed wide with ornate iron spindles, rather impressive.

'I live on the top floor.' Smith bounded upwards. A door banged down below, but nobody emerged. Now they took to a second, wooden, narrow flight of stairs closed in on both sides by blank, tall walls. 'Servants' quarters.'

'What's the date?'

'Eighteen-fifties, I think, though I'm not sure. Deeds are incomplete.'

'It's not Regency, then?'

'No. It's not unlike in some ways, but builders here were right behind the times. Sit down.'

They entered a large room with a desk by the long window, armchairs, two settees, bookshelves, laden tables, a plethora of pictures. Smith went out and Worth could hear him at the coffee-mill. 'It was a regular rabbit warren up here, floors on all sorts of levels,' the host called back in. 'I rationalized it.'

Worth took to one of the easy chairs, dug his heels into the Wilton carpet and eyed three John Pipers over his right arm. To his left an untidy tower of books piled, one of four. He lifted off the top volume, N.R. Murphy's *The Interpretation of Plato's Republic*, and opened it idly. 'The Definition of Justice', 'The Parts of the Soul'. He closed it, and with it his eyes.

'Shan't be a moment now,' Smith shouted.

The room spoke affluence, for though there might be dust in the corners, the furniture was substantial, unveneered, well looked after. The covers on the broad settees had been laundered within the week; two late eighteenth-century round-topped tables were bordered with matching chairs. Smith brought in a tray.

'Care for a biscuit?' he asked.

'No, thanks.'

'I'm a provision merchant. I can recommend these.'

'No, thank you.'

Inquiries made about milk and sugar, Smith poured the coffee, into excellent large china cups.

'Pleasant up here.' Worth felt the need to be sociable.

'I get the heat from the people below. We warm up too much in summer just under the roof, but I'm out of the way, with plenty of room and a good view.' From where he sat Worth seemed to look out over the top of a forest, an uneven green floor of leaves punctuated by gables. 'The whole house is too big, and besides I like the sounds of occupation. I've an office here. I needn't go out.' He led Worth towards a door behind which were phones, a bank of files, a typewriter, a dictating apparatus, and a box of tricks with a television screen. 'My computer.'

'You've premises elsewhere?'

'Warser Gate. Purefoy Street. And in Mansfield, Leicester, Derby, Chesterfield, Sheffield, Manchester. Even London. I say it myself, but sometimes I work very hard.'

'You read a lot?'

'I pretend to. That's not the same thing.' He sighed, windily, then supped his coffee in silence. 'I collect pictures, but I don't know what I'm doing.' He spun in his chair to extract and unwrap a sketch from his desk, a small scribble, a preliminary perhaps for *The Pipes of Pan*, two young men in loincloths, with Spanish features.

'Picasso,' Worth said. 'And I thought you said I was too expensive.'

'I was pulling your leg.' He allowed Worth to hold and study the paper in front of him. 'Now why should I like that?'

'I don't know. I can't answer for you.'

'But why should I regard that highly?' Puzzlingly ambiguous. 'What's good about it?'

'You paid a lot of money for it, for a start.'

'Don't give me that.' He sounded angry, genuinely so.

'It should interest you and go on encouraging you to look at it, and think about it, and remember it, and be touched or troubled or pleased about it.'

'But that's not necessarily aesthetic, is it? It might be that I like the story, or the figures sexually arouse me, or it reminds me of my circumstances when I bought it.'

'That will have to do, then. If that's the interest you find in pictures, then it's neither too bad, nor too unusual either, even in those who are supposed to know about art.'

'But a very poor picture from a chocolate box or a calendar might do as well?'

'Thank God,' Worth said. 'It won't cost you so much.'

'Are you serious?' Smith clutched his chin with his left hand, enthusiastically, like a sixth-former debating.

Worth handed the sketch back, and pronounced as if it seemed expected. 'I don't care much for it, really. The problems that he's trying to solve here aren't those that worry me. Moreover he's solved them years ago, and they've become clichés; that is, they've been copied by every second-, third-, fourth-rate dauber and commercial hack for the last, oh, fifty years, so that I can't see the thing with an innocent eye. If I'd been there with the man on the morning he'd dashed it off, and I knew what he was obsessed with, and what others he scribbled out as soon as he'd done this, it might interest me more. But this bit of paper means very little as far as I'm concerned.'

'I might as well chuck it in the fire.'

'You'd be a bloody fool, but yes.'

'You don't like Picasso?' Smith pressed.

'Picasso's a dozen, a score of artists. That's why he impresses me. Like a whirlwind. A force of nature. Different from us plodders.'

'Wouldn't that be true of Rembrandt, or Raphael or any great . . . ?'

'Yes.' Worth interrupted the sentence because he had lost interest in the argument and he'd thought of Vermeer. Smith, apparently understanding, reached out and refilled his guest's cup. They sat in companionable silence, almost as if they had completed a round in the boxing ring, where though each had learnt much of his opponent, neither had gleaned enough. And yet to Worth's mind there was nothing antagonistic, or competitive, between them.

'Do you not work on Sundays?' he asked, willing to repay hospitality with words.

'As often as not. If there's nothing more interesting. It's either that or the whisky bottle.'

'Aren't you married?' That impertinence seemed right for this man in this room.

'No. I have been. Twice. Once widowed, once divorced. You're a bachelor, aren't you? I always thought of you as not liking women, doing your marvellous detailed painting where there were no women about, no clashes and temptations of the flesh,' he laughed, 'no . . . Not even homosexual. Neuter for art.'

'How did you arrive at these bizarre conclusions?' Taken aback and bridling.

'Made them up.' Smith was in no way abashed. 'I'd seen photographs of you. Denzil Reaper's last exhibition had six or seven of you at work.'

'I'm not like them?'

'Yes, you are. In so far as I'd recognize you from them. But you're more solid. Not earthy, ashy somehow. Rough. Not creamy. Not misty. You're a funny bugger.'

'Thank you.'

'I can see you don't like this. I don't blame you. Some stranger invites you in to boast and air his grievances and waste your time and then insults you. Do you ever feel you're getting nowhere?'

'Almost always.'

'That's a comfort. But you'll leave something behind.'

'Won't you? Shops. Money.'

'Shares in supermarkets. Great God.' Smith's face was not displeased, redly grinning. 'I'm glad I met you. When I saw you sketching away there, I thought to myself, "There's somebody actually doing something, not traipsing round the street waiting for something to happen." Could I look?' He pointed towards

103

the satchel at Worth's feet. The books were extracted, handed over, glanced at, rather too curiously, the artist thought. 'You'll work on these, I take it. Would you sell me one or two then? As a memento? When you've done with them, of course.'

Worth shrugged.

'I'll see what comes of it,' he answered. He did not want to think of the sketches just then, but felt under obligation to his host. He began, surprising himself, an account of his attempts at the mural for the London house. Smith, pouring more coffee, lighting himself a cigar, listened in comfortable lethargy, his weight wringing creaks from his wide chair.

'Interesting,' he said. 'And you thought this morning's fracas would . . . ?'

'Thought? Yes.'

'Has it?'

'That I don't know. Now, you tell me what you'd paint on an Arab prince's wall.'

Edwin Smith seemed to take that seriously.

'Describe the room again.' Worth did so. 'Yes. And you don't know anything about the man? What is he? Royalty? Oilty?'

Worth confessed ignorance, but meticulously characterized Walden, the go-between. As the one talked, the other leaning back even more expansively, legs at full, fat stretch, rubbed his belly, exploring it with fingers as if he could conjure an answer from the rotundity. He hummed, a deep note, as from a spinning-top, an accompaniment to the spidering of his fingers. 'Something English, I should have thought. A park. Trees. A lake. Horse or two. Ladies and gentlemen in eighteenth-century dress and afternoon sunshine. A mansion at a discreet distance.'

'Pastiche?'

'I suppose so.' Smith seemed surprised at the resentment in the word. 'A window into the past.' He laughed, a forced chuckle. 'No good, eh? You say this foyer's a touch dark, do you? Well, Wright of Derby, then. The experiment. With the candlelight. Air out of a bell jar with the bird in it. Faces. And the moon clouded outside the window. Think of those faces on the wall, all tied up in their concerns.'

'Skinheads by petrol-bomb light?'

'Could be. He did another odd thing. Boys fighting over a bladder.'

Someone gently tapped at a panel, then pushed the door open before Smith could offer an invitation to enter.

A fair-headed young woman, with a striking figure, not pretty, swerved in.

'Hello. You've got visitors.' She was in no way discomfited.

'Make some more coffee, Jo,' Smith ordered.

'I shall have to be leaving.' Worth's objection.

'This,' said Smith with formality, 'is the distinguished painter John Worth.'

Jo frowned, running fingers into her curls. 'Bridge with leaning trees. In your bedroom,' she said. 'Burwell Park.'

'Sounds bad.' Smith. 'Josephine Feaver.' She nodded, picked up the coffeepot and made for the kitchen. 'One of my tenants,' Smith said, not lowering his voice. 'One of my long-standing clients. An artistic lady.'

'Say no more,' Jo shouted from the kitchen.

'How long have you lived here?' Worth asked the host.

'Three years.' He described the buying of the house, the alterations which made the place uninhabitable for a year – he'd lived in one room and a lavatory – and then his decision to let rooms or floors out. 'I'm away a fair amount. I'm going to Melbourne this week. So I'd either to close the house and let the damp in, or have tenants here who'd ruin my paintwork.'

'Why didn't you sell the place at a profit if it was inconvenient?' Worth.

'He likes company,' Jo said, not shouting, but crystal clear from the kitchen. 'And somebody to bully.'

'But isn't it difficult once you've taken people on to get rid of them?'

'Not for him,' Jo said. 'He'd squirt CS gas under your doors.'

Smith leaned back, supporting his head with knitted hands, happy with the comment.

'Hurry up with that bloody coffee,' he called, and drew Worth's attention to a small Henry Moore drawing of a sheep which he'd bought twelve months ago as a birthday present, but had never given away. 'I don't like it either, but I was unnaturally pleased when I gave the girl a leather handbag instead.'

'Mean sod,' Jo muttered, without.

'I wanted to impress her. I mean I would have told her what I paid for it, but I couldn't hand it over, in the end. So I bought her one of these hand-tooled, artistic pieces of fine leathercraft on my travels, and she was satisfied. I couldn't bring myself to waste that Moore on her. What do you think?'

'Good for Henry Moore,' Worth said.

This brought Jo Feaver back to the door, arms out, palms flat on the uprights.

'Don't you believe it,' she said. 'He's a bastard to women.'

'To you?' Worth.

'And any other daft enough to open her legs for him.'

She disappeared. Smith stood, took down the sheep, looked hard at it himself and passed it to Worth. This occupied them until Jo's return.

'More coffee, John?' she asked, lifting his cup. Her mouth was wide. She poured from a height. 'Give us a ciggie,' she ordered Smith. He opened a mahogany box from which she picked a black, gold-tipped exotic object, which she lit for herself.

'Aren't you smoking?' she demanded of Smith.

'Not today.' He pointed at his cigar butt in the ashtray.

She affected a sneer, threw herself onto a settee, crossed bare, excellent legs, exposing one to the top of the thigh.

'What's he doing to you?' she asked Worth.

'I'm preventing him from working on his sketches by providing this Italian coffee,' Smith answered. 'Creating works of art consists of an artist's placing obstacles in his own way, and then trying to surmount them. I'm saving Mr Worth the job. I'm stopping him. Holding him down here, so that he'll be bursting to begin by the time he escapes.'

'He might have gone off the boil,' she said. Again she threw her pretty legs round.

'In which case there'd have been little to get excited about.'

'How do you know?' she asked.

106

'Pictures aren't painted by chance,' Smith said. 'As you well know.'

'Thus spoke the prophet.' She finished her coffee, black, and pushed herself vigorously upwards to refill her cup. 'Anybody else?' She turned to Worth again. 'He loves to pronounce,' she said. 'He ought to have been a schoolteacher.' She straightened her face as she lifted the cup from which she did not drink. 'Get him to give you a commission.'

'This man is under orders for a mural from Saudi royalty or some oil potentate. What chance have I got?'

Her eyes opened wide, and when Worth was invited to go over the story again, he was not bored.

12

In the middle of the week, when the weather had become hotter, drying out the sandy soil of his garden, Worth returned from a trying hour with Theodore Turnbull in a public park. He had never liked Mansthorpe Grange much, a small uneven strip of land, with a miniature golf course and the rest of the grass occupied by screaming boys playing cricket or quarrelling over the game. The pair had parked the car in the road outside, and walked uphill along what had been an avenue of elms, now ugly stumps. Turnbull made painful work of the progress, sighing, halting, complaining about undisciplined youth, staggering on again, wishing vehemently he were back at home. He had refused to take a stick, huffily grunting he was not an old man, but he had now reduced his companion to sweating anger and himself to near imbecility. Worth parked him on a seat, uncomfortable, with splinters, and offered to fetch an ice-cream. This was refused with contumely. They watched a boy ape some Test bowler capering a thirty-yard run-up, and this led to a lecture on fast bowling, the value of example, its counterfeit opposite; nothing could be as good as it had been. A slash towards cover point smacked the ball dangerously into one of the legs of their seat, and though a fielder apologized reluctantly and awkwardly, Turnbull led off again: youth, age, manners, training, craven parenthood, an incompetent teaching profession. Worth was relieved to lead his friend back to the car, which Teddy, now purged, drove like a man in vigorous middle age without a word against road hogs, motor-cyclists, corporation busmen or dithering women. He thanked Worth, shook hands, closed the gate across his drive singing.

John Worth sat at home, knowing he should either prepare a meal or begin to work, but too despondent to start either. Once he began to paint his tiredness might well disappear, but he seemed incapable of mastering his inertia. The ringing of the phone jerked him out of his miserable lassitude.

'Jo Feaver.' He did not answer. 'We met last Sunday at Eddie Smith's.'

'Yes.' Dull, dull.

'Am I interrupting anything? Don't be afraid to say, now.'

'No.'

'Can I come round to see you?'

'When?'

'Now, if you like. Any time to please you.'

'Is it important?'

'Of course it isn't. Why the hell should it be?' He'd no idea whether she joked, but there was a hardness in her voice. 'I'm at a loose end.'

'Aren't you at work?'

'Not today.'

'Come round now, then.'

She arrived an hour later, smiling, fit for the summer in a simple cream dress with silver high-heeled shoes. Her fair hair was elaborately uncombed and her brown hands free of rings.

'I rang on impulse,' she announced, sitting primly back in an armchair. 'That's not quite true, but it'll do for a start.' Her teeth were even as she smiled. 'Eddie, Edwin, has gone off to London today, and flies to Australia tomorrow. We've talked about you twice since the weekend.' That sounded as if it meant something. 'We didn't quite make head or tail of you, and so he told me to get round and quiz you again. That's typical of him. He hates delay. He does everything energetically, on the spur of the moment. Like snatching you off the street. And if there'd been nothing to you, you'd have been out of his back gate quick as the dustbin.'

'What was so interesting about me?'

'You paint. He knew of you. And you seemed a secretive man, a creeper round the corners.' She laughed at her own phrase. 'More in you than meets the eye.'

'I see.'

He inquired about refreshment; she chose iced lemonade.

'All this came out in the two conversations?' Worth asked sarcastically, as they settled again.

'That and more.' She lifted her glass to him. ' "Get round and talk to him," he said, "and if you like him, I'll commission a portrait of you." Just like that.'

'Have you any idea what a portrait would cost?' He spoke aggressively.

'That's what I asked Edwin. Straight off.'

'And what did he say?'

' "Worth's a good provincial, who sells quite well in London, but he's not gone out of his tiny mind yet, so," ' she seemed to be imitating Smith's boom admirably, without deepening her own voice, ' "if he painted somebody locally, and it went without snags, it would be um, um, a thousand, thirteen hundred at the outside." Is that right?'

He nodded. 'Not bad.' He looked her over. 'Mr Smith would spend a thousand pounds having a portrait made of you?'

'It's nothing to him. He's filthy with it. Besides, ordinary people think nothing of blueing a thousand, several thousands, bringing their car up to date. He'd spend it on art, and say how cheap it was even compared with just the running of his Rolls. Would you do it?'

'I'd have to consider it.'

'Right then. Start your consideration. Do you get many commissions? I know you have this Arab thing.'

'No.'

'I realize you're looking at me, but you should be asking me some questions.'

'Why?'

'To get to know what I'm like, so you can deal with my character.' She mocked him. 'Do you see me as beautiful?'

'Interesting.'

'That's something.' She now stared at him, challenging him to do something about it, her.

'Why is it,' he began, 'that Smith would pay a considerable sum of money to have you painted? If he wanted another picture of mine, he could buy one for less, and he'd see what he was buying. This might be unsatisfactory. Where do you come in?'

'Forget the considerable sum,' she said. 'A thousand pounds is chickenfeed to him.'

'I've usually found that rich people don't fling their money about. That's why they're rich.'

'Art's his hobby. And boats.'

'What about you, then?'

'Why does he want a picture of me, do you mean? What's my hold over him? I just happened to be there at the time. Chance. Luck. We hit it off. He's . . . How old do you think he is?'

'Thirty-eight. Forty.'

'He's fifty.' The same age as Theodore Turnbull.

'He doesn't look it.'

'I have a small pad in his house. I rent it. We've screwed, but who hasn't? I'm not his grand passion, if that's what you imagine, but he'll do me a good turn if he can.'

'Who'll keep the picture when it's finished?'

'Good question. He will, if it's any good. Do you do sketches? He'll buy one or two of them and put 'em in silver frames for me.'

'You're on to a profitable line,' Worth said, not knowing why.

Jo Feaver twisted her rugged features in distaste, so that for a moment he thought she would launch blistering insults his way, but she dispersed anger with a florid wave of her hands, spoke in an even voice. 'Edwin says that you're not going to get that

Arab commission. They're messing you about. The Hungarian or whoever he is.'

'How does he know that?'

'He doesn't. He's shrewd, but he's guessing. He reckons that Walden has put the job out to half a dozen of you. To talented people, so he can't go wrong. He pleases you all, and he makes a packet spending time on you.'

'And the others are better than I am?' Worth asked.

'Not necessarily. But you won't put yourself about.' She raised a hand against his protest. 'Not at bottom. You think you're going to all sorts of trouble with your vandals and riots and executions but, this is what Edwin says, and I agree, there is about you a thus-far-and-no-farther. You confine yourself and your talents and your objectives within certain limits, and nothing's going to push you outside those.'

'Is that good or bad?'

'It's the key point about any artist. He knows what he can and will do. With great painters the limits are on the whole wide, not subject matter exactly, but treatment. One can be confined to self-portraits, say, or interiors, and still be marvellously, universally varied.'

'And in my case?' He did not know how he dared ask this.

'Ah. Well, that's it.' She looked about, in a flurry of bird-like panic, perhaps to escape. When finally she spoke it was slowly, every consonant lucid. 'Edwin said, "John Worth's a man waiting to become famous, instead of going out to chase fame." He meant that you're painting what you want, not what will catch the eye of the public.'

'I think that's a compliment.'

'He didn't mean it as such. He's sure you have talent, but he thinks that, given that, you should draw attention to yourself. What's the use of fame to you when you're dead? You should throw your pot of paint in the face of the public, and that doesn't mean you need do pot-boiling rubbish. Look at fashion.'

'I have done. That's why I go my own road.'

'No, it isn't,' she argued. 'You'll tell me that nobody knows what people in a hundred years will look on as great. You'll add

111

that if you hit the jackpot now with your contemporaries, it's quite likely you'll be out of favour in twenty years, if not less. But I answer you in two ways.'

'Go on.'

'One, you act as you do because of your personality. I call it a defect; you a strength. The second thing, and it ties up with the first, is that if you did become famous, there'd be furious stresses and strains on you which might be rotten for you, but ideal for your work. Or vice versa. You don't want that.'

'I'll give you this, you can lay down the law.'

'I've a degree in fine art.'

'Oh, Christ. Is that what you do for a living?'

'No. Oh, no.' Her teeth met, fretted the lower lip. 'I work for a computer firm now.'

'But not today?' he asked.

'I'm taking two days' holiday. To let you have a look at me. But we're not here to discuss my case. You haven't answered me. Why don't you make the effort to be famous?'

'I don't know how.' He rubbed his left hand up the bristles of his left cheek. 'It's mostly luck or other people who do the trick for you. But if I knew, I'm not sure I'd do it, because at the ground and bottom of your reasoning is a fallacy. And it's this.' He stopped, wagged a finger at her as if to make sure of her unsplit attention. 'Just because I doddle along here, dull as ditchwater, it doesn't mean nothing's happening to me. It's the constant attention I pay that counts. I'm for ever on the edge of expectancy, for good or bad.'

'Go on.' She leaned back with a flurry of beautiful crossed legs.

'If somebody took me up on the TV, or if I appeared myself and made some sort of hit, then I'd sell more pictures and I could put my prices up. But it seems spurious, factitious. And it would take the edge off my, well, my reaction to the world. I don't want to be splashing words like "sensitivity" about; I'd be as bad as the posh Sunday writers. But that's it. As I am now, the law of diminishing returns doesn't work.'

'Because you start off in such a low key.'

'That's how it appears to you. Not to me.'

112

'What awful, terrifying thing has happened to you, then?'
She pounced.

'My girl committed suicide.' He answered, unhesitatingly, like a confident card-player.

'When?'

'Five years ago.'

'Why?'

'How do I know? Why does anybody kill herself? The world was too much for her?'

'And you blame yourself.' Jo's voice was softer.

'I can't help thinking I could have done better. It surprised me, caught me out utterly, because . . . I didn't think she'd do it, though she threatened often enough.'

'Will you tell me her name?'

'Monica Pilgrim. Does that mean anything to you?'

'No. Except a name always does carry weight. Even if it had been Jane Smith or Mary Brown. I'm rotten at remembering names, because they seem so important. You don't want to tell me about her?'

'No.'

'It would lose its power, do you think? For you?'

'I don't want to talk about her. Stop.'

'But you'll have to think about her, won't you, now I've dragged it up?'

'I don't need your help for that, thank you.'

'She's always in your mind?'

'I forget her for weeks on end, sometimes. And I can remember, in words, what it was like. My body seemed reduced to a metal tube, incapable of movement. That, and a chronic nausea.'

'Did it stop your work?'

'Yes. I did my best, but I did nothing worth anything over a period, of, oh, six months.'

'I see.' She sounded solemn, but as suddenly her mood switched, she grinned. 'Are you going to make a sketch of me, then?' He, wrapped in his thoughts, kept silence, his mouth sagging slightly open, his eyes squinting, hands trembling. 'You can charge it to Edwin.'

113

'All right,' he mumbled.

'Good,' she said, 'good,' and sprang from her chair. 'Do we work here or in your studio?'

'I'll do pencil sketches. Perhaps a few photographs. It's more comfortable in here.'

'Is comfort a concomitant of art?' she probed, as he walked out. The word 'concomitant' rang gong-like, cheering, summoning to a feast, so that he felt lifted.

Returning he said out loud, clearly, 'Order, luxury, calm,' but she had forgotten, was engaged elsewhere, preparing herself to be caught on paper.

He opened his book, weighed his pencil, one of six, looked hard at her, then asked her to move. She obeyed, but objected, 'This feels unnatural.'

'We're trying things out,' he answered pacifically. 'You're learning to be a model, for one thing.'

'Do I need to sit stock still?'

'If you can.'

'Have you started yet? I can't see you.'

'No. Shan't be long. Surely you did some life classes on your fine arts course?'

'I'd sooner forget about them.' She turned her head to smile brilliantly at him, then swung it back, perched stiffly, holding her breath. Worth had begun, not tentatively, rapidly about it, tongue between teeth.

After something like a quarter of an hour, he invited her to look. 'Stand up,' he said, 'get out of your seat and relax.'

Her face, in three-quarter profile, was delicately completed, while the back of her head was suggested, by a thin, cunning outline. In the top right-hand corner of the large page were two rapid sketches of her nose, and below the neck, a quick scribble of her lips and lower chin.

'You've caught the likeness,' she said.

'Yes,' he admitted.

'I seem puzzled. As if I'm frowning at something.'

'And you weren't?'

'I wanted to make my mind a blank. An orange blur.'

'Let's try again.'

114

This time, he did a full-face portrait, or two, the first a mere arbitrary choice of a few lines, not caricature so much as an indication of intention, a shorthand note of her position in space, a lovely reduction. The second employed shading, loomed darker, and yet took nothing away from her fairness of hair, pale-brown skin, flash of blue eyes.

'That's marvellous,' she pronounced.

'But wrong.'

'Why do you say that?'

'It's art-school stuff,' he said.

'Did you win many prizes at college?'

'No end. For doing as I was told.'

'That's how artists learn.'

'Oh, sure, sure. And you'll never be any good unless you learn that. But if you stick there you're dead. That's the awful thing. There's this lottery that fashion will take you up and throw you down without rhyme or reason, then the responsibility to yourself of learning standards, and growing, building.'

'I think these are very good,' she said. 'Look at that.' She pointed at the first of the full-face sketches. 'It's economical. Very few marks on the paper, and every one counting.'

'You think so because you're prepared to read into my scratches more than is there. Other artists scribble hundreds and dozens of lines and you pick out the ones you want.'

'Your code convinces me, you mean,' Josephine objected.

'It's useless talking about drawing,' he said.

'Can I come again?' She exhibited schoolgirl enthusiasm, unfitted to her elegant appearance, and after he had arranged a sitting, she cradled his hand in both of hers.

13

During two weeks of August Worth gave perhaps half a dozen sittings to Josephine Feaver, and spent a third week in a scorched Derbyshire. On his return he found a note from Millicent Turnbull informing him that her husband had been taken into hospital. The note, typically, he thought, mentioned neither the name of the hospital nor the cause; she claimed she had several times tried to reach him by telephone and had concluded that he was away. She asked if he would 'get in touch' immediately he returned. Amongst the other letters there was nothing from Walden, nor from Edwin Smith who would discuss, Jo averred, terms with the artist immediately he returned from Australia and the Far East. There were bills, no cheques, and a mishmash of advertising material.

For two days he tried to ring Millicent, but she seemed never at home, and by the third day the quest had become a kind of desperate game. If Turnbull were in dock, then it was possible she was staying with friends, but it seemed unlikely; his son, Piers, could be expected to turn up and need catering for. Worth made a worried expedition to the house, hammered on the door, peered through the windows, searched round the back. There were few signs of recent occupation; he noted that Millicent had done nothing about the redecoration of the drawing room. No one had cut the lawn for some weeks, and the pot piants on the patio were bone dry and dying; he turned on the hose, still attached to the outside tap and lying haphazardly in the yard, and soaked them. By the kitchen window were two unwashed cups, and on the inside sill of the breakfast room a notice, fading, almost indecipherable in the bright sunlight and at an awkward angle. He determined to read the damned thing before he left; his future, that of Theodore Turnbull, of Millicent, the mural, the universe depended on it. He peered through the dusty pane, picking up a letter here, there. The first word he made out was 'November', then 'gibbet', 'giblet', how did one spell these outlandish exoticisms? 'Gilbert', but where was the companion phrase 'and Sullivan'? Nowhere. It would be some cyclostyled affair from Turnbull's school. He tried to recall names of the Savoy operas, to fit them to the hieroglyphics; his frustration seethed that in this sharp sunlight he could understand so little. In the end, he rang the doorbells of the houses on either side, and stood there unanswered. This was the holiday season so that he could hardly expect people to stay at home to please him, but he was riled. He searched through his pockets for a pencil to leave a note; the sun blazed down. He found a sketch-block, but nothing to write with. Bloody artist who swans about without visible means of making a mark. He kicked over a moribund, potted geranium.

At 10.30, he was listening to the radio in bed. Millicent telephoned, breathlessly.

'I'm glad I've caught you. I've been trying for more than a week.' He explained his absence, and described that morning's call. 'I wondered who'd been round,' she said. 'I didn't think the Fernleighs would have noticed anything needed watering, or Piers, if he'd been.' She seemed both excited and disorganized as she told him how Theodore had suddenly become worse, deeply depressed, weeping, almost incapable of movement and had been taken into St Mary's. There they had put him out so that he barely recognized her, was lost in a kind of waking sleep, though just about capable of eating. 'The doctor says he'll be miles better when he comes round, but he won't remember.' The weeks under drugs would be excised from his life.

'They advised me to have a holiday, and I rang a girl I knew at the Poly and she invited me over. It was in Stoke-on-Trent, but she really looked after me. I never got up before midday. And I ate like a horse. She pampered me. She's just got her degree and is going to college for a year to study for her Law Society exams.' Millicent flung facts about as if it were a pleasure to talk, a relief. Perhaps, he guessed, she'd thought he'd be embarrassed, but that was wrong; she paid no attention to him, she sloshed him with words like someone washing down a yard, knowing there was little need of close scrutiny of the effect. In the end, at five past eleven, she invited him to accompany her to the hospital, insisted on using her car, told him exactly when she would collect him. She rang off, laughing, as if she'd arranged a treat.

When she knocked at his back door the following afternoon, five minutes early, she wore a light, not very clean, mackintosh and a hât, which, though small, seemed to make her older, staid, unrecognizable. In no way subdued, she led him out to her car, chatting sociably, making it clear to him that he must not expect recognition from Turnbull, that it would all be boring, that they would not stay long, but that somehow she felt her appearance after an absence would somehow cheer her husband. What she said seemed neither logical nor even necessary, merely words to fill an embarrassing gap.

St Mary's was small, a series of three low, parallel brick buildings fingering out from a larger block, all neat, with a border of holly and rhododendron, outlined by strips of grass and ageratum, with gravel paths, a large display of hybrid tea roses by the main gate and a thin wall between the hospital and the busy road. They drove in but, finding the available places full or for use of medical staff, had to trickle out to park on the avenue, decent middle-range, middle-class houses, at the side of the hospital.

'It's an odd spot, this,' he commented, insecure.

'I imagine it was a piece of spare ground as near to the main buildings as they could get.'

'It might be a light-engineering factory,' he said. 'Was it built after the war?'

'I'm not sure. I think it might date from the thirties.'

They reported at a desk inside the ward behind which a middle-aged man in a white coat with a name tag nodded absently and pointed. 'You know where he is,' he said.

'How is he?'

'Much the same. You won't notice much difference while he's still under treatment.'

'But it usually works?'

Another white-coated figure entered, handed the first a sheet or two of typing.

'Some of the results are miraculous,' the man answered her, flat as a pancake, pushing his bifocals higher on his nose to read the papers.

They walked the length of the ward, with chintzy curtains, and pastel colours. The beds were neatly made up, and mostly unoccupied, though here and there a man sat in a chair.

'Not many patients,' Worth said.

'The place is packed. They send them down to the recreation rooms.'

'All walking wounded,' he answered foolishly. She seemed to stagger, away from him or the remark. A balding man, seated by his bedside reading a book, looked at them, and responded to Worth's greeting, a good omen.

'In here,' she said, ushering him through the open door of a private room, pleasantly windowed, brighter than the ward. Turnbull lay with eyes closed, hands above the counterpane. In this position his face seemed bloated, and though reddish still, paler than the outdoor man's. 'Hello, darling,' she said, sitting, kissing, touching the patient. 'How are you, then? Look who's come to see you.' Turnbull opened his eyes, slowly; it was like bad acting, and he made a soft sound in their direction, before he shut himself away again.

Millicent tidied sheets and pillows, set out fruit, unpacking her bag to pile towels, underwear and pyjamas on the end of the cot, before ransacking the cupboards for soiled linen. All the time she talked, inquiring if her husband felt better, whether they were looking after him properly and following this with spirited information about the trip to Stoke-on-Trent. Worth admired her; the quiet voice never faltered, maintained cheerfulness, brought to the hospital an everyday, undeniable comfort. The fact that Turnbull stirred only sluggishly, answered in a mumble, barely mustered a change of expression did nothing to deter her. Now she chirruped on how clean the towels were, and she hoped that they were keeping him washed and decent. At twenty-three years of age she seemed in command, knowing exactly what the situation required, providing it.

How adequately she coped was clearer when, judging he had become accustomed to the place, she introduced Worth into the conversation. He shuffled forward, awkwardly took hold of one of Turnbull's hands which was warm, normal, and asked how things were going, made stilted remarks about the room, the outlook, the weather. It is true that Turnbull attempted to answer, not altogether unintelligibly, so that the effort was not

119

wasted, but Worth found the going impossible. He did his best with the current Test series, but could not remember yesterday's score; he tried to recall some interesting snippet he'd read about the county rugby team's approaching season, and failed. When Millicent joined in again, he turned his back on the bed pretending to examine the room and its fixtures and then stood at a window urgently scanning a wide, urban landscape.

They stayed a boring forty-five minutes; the ward, the desk, the corridor, the dusty shrubs were heavenly compared with that cell, the dead-and-alive man on whom the girl desperately had worked her wits, lovingly, for so little return. She refused to join Worth for tea, telling him he was too busy, thanked him effusively, said she would keep in touch and drove off, head proud. He spent the evening down in an armchair in front of the television, incapable of action, numb.

He attended hospital three times with her in the next week, and saw the improvement in Turnbull's condition. On the final occasion, the patient had been up and dressed, sat with them in a commonroom, rather similar to a school hall, with rows of chairs stacked by the walls, except for those bunched in front of the television set, and had finally ventured out for ten minutes of fresh air with them in the grounds. The man appeared normal, talked like himself, grumbled but within reason, though just before he returned indoors he stood at the gate watching the not very heavy afternoon traffic, and there was puzzlement written on his face, paralysis, as though the swishing by of a saloon car, the thump on a grate of a lorry, the braking of a bus at the stop was too much for his comprehension. Back home Worth tried to catch the expression in a sketch of his friend; he drew a zombie, a soulless being. Turnbull had stood there like the man-in-the-street translated to Mars.

That evening Millicent called round, for no reason that he could see, talked of her husband's recovery, praised hospital and treatment, and genially speaking burst into tears. She soon recovered, dabbing at her face with a crumpled tissue, but he knew what these last weeks had cost her. She had continued at work, had driven up to St Mary's at least once a day, had come back to an empty house full of Teddy's books and trophies, to

120

do his laundry. Neither Piers nor Natalie Ball had made an appearance, though Elspeth, who must have heard of his second breakdown through her daughter, wrote an awkward, presumably sympathetic, letter to Turnbull, full of a holiday she had spent in Egypt, making one slighting reference to Milly.

'You've done very well,' Worth said.

Millicent did not even glance up at him. She sat straight, face unlined, dark spots of tears on her blouse, a damp tissue crumpled in a clenched hand. She looked young, no older than one of Teddy's sixth-formers, pretty enough, neat now and calm, but Worth knew inside himself an immense surge of joy at what she had done, this ordinary girl, was doing still. She had no idea of her accomplishment, would have been ashamed if he tried to explain it or his reaction to it, but he was lifted, soberly and fiercely, so he perched high on his chair, typically ignoring, paying no attention to her, the source of his emotion.

They had a second cup of coffee some minutes later when she apologized for her behaviour, but he took and held her hand, so that the pair stood in the middle of the room, reflected in his mother's old mantel mirror, she slightly embarrassed, patting her hair straight, he out of his commonplace conventionality, out of character, a new man with no notion of how to conduct, or construe, himself, hand in hand, without sexual urge, with this young woman, lady, girl, genius of humane wit. He took her to the studio to show her the pencil sketches of Jo Feaver, the first one in oils, and the beginnings of a formal portrait.

That restored the humdrum.

Millicent immediately commented and questioned. Jo wasn't pretty, but she seemed lively. Is that how he saw her? Elegant, oh? Then if she was so, why hadn't he done a full portrait instead of head and shoulders? Was she attractive in her speech, manners? Clever? The girl grew buoyant with these questions, laughing, dashing her hands about.

'What does Ursula think of her?' she asked.

'She doesn't know she exists.'

'That's suspicious.' Woman's magazine. 'Why haven't you told her?'

'I've not seen much of her lately.'

'I'm sorry. Do you know, I thought you were in love with Ursula Quinn. I really did.'

'And was she in love with me?' He was half serious with the question.

'I don't know. I guessed so, but there's no evidence. Or for you, either. You're not like adolescents cuddling at the bus stops, are you? I mean, you're not very demonstrative and she's forceful, almost mannish. I don't mean anything wrong; I mean, she's very feminine and very beautiful, but she speaks up for herself. That would have been good for you.'

'She thinks I've no interest in politics.'

'Is that true?'

'Something in it, sure. She wants my pictures to have political content.'

'Has she always been like that?'

'Politically inclined, yes. Went along to her teachers' union and spoke. Member of the Labour Party. That sort of thing. But she's moved leftwards, thinks the country's going fascist, becoming a police state.'

'Is it?'

'Not as far as I can see. But I'm an anaemic liberal, small *l*.'

'Why has she changed, then? She seems sensible, what little I've had to do with her.'

'She's got in with the group led by a chap named Stout, Stuart Stout. He's a city councillor now.'

'I saw her walking hand in hand with him along Gladstone Street,' Millicent said, and caught her breath, 'last week. He's a married man, isn't he?'

'No idea. Yes, I think he is, because I've heard his wife's name bandied about in the local rag.'

'Philomena Stout.' This girl knew more than she had let on. Troubled, he wondered if she had begun the evening with the intention of mentioning Ursula. 'With that name she'll be a Catholic.'

'What's that to the purpose?'

'He won't get a divorce.' Her eyes opened wide. 'I know people don't seem to bother so much about that, these days.'

'No.' Annoyed with himself, he realized her news had cut deeply. True, he had not seen Ursula, had taken it that she had lost interest, but he did not want chapter and verse from independent witnesses.

'I'm sorry,' Millicent said. 'Perhaps I oughtn't to have . . . ' She returned to his pictures of Jo Feaver, tried to joke about their political content.

'Ursula would tell you,' he waved at the unfinished oil, 'that it had plenty. Of the wrong sort. Fascist, sexist rubbish, opiate of the people, hardly better than Bunnyclubs, Playboy, page three of the *Sun*.'

Uncomfortable now, she explained why she had to leave at once, what thousand and one chores she needed to complete before bed. She shook hands, dazed, pale, withdrawn; she ought to have more on her mind than his love life. Immediately she had gone, he rang the Quinns.

Edgar Quinn answered. No, Urs'la wasn't in. She'd be on one of these political dos, or parent–teachers', 'You know what she's like.' He hadn't heard much of Worth recently. 'You haven't been round. Saw a thing in the paper about some picture of yours.' Pressed for details, Edgar was morosely vague, and Worth made no sense of the item, which he had not read. 'I'll tell her, though, when she gets back.'

As always Quinn worked hard to return to doing nothing.

Two days later Ursula appeared at eight o'clock when he was eating his cooked meal. He had spent the daylight hours on Jo's portrait, and the rest on experiments with the sketches brought back from Derbyshire. *The Entry into Jerusalem* had been abandoned, with the executions and the riots.

She accepted a piece of cold apple pie, complained there was no custard and dowsed it in milk-bottle top. He found her remarkably like her father on these occasions.

'You rang up,' she said, mouth full. 'Was it anything important?'

'I hadn't heard from you recently.'

'It may not have struck you that some of us have our living to earn. The schools have started again.' Vulgarly she pushed away her dish, a heap of pie crust untasted. 'What are you up to?'

When he described his work, she demanded to be taken to the studio, but he poured himself more tea. Ursula questioned him about Walden, and, informed he'd heard nothing, began a diatribe, instructing him to ring the Burden gallery, issue ultimatums, dress 'em down, stand up for himself. He listened without comment, manoeuvring the crumbs on the tablecloth into uninteresting patterns, until she took umbrage about that.

'Stop fidgeting,' she said. 'Say something.'

'I've already been told that I'm waiting to become famous instead of doing something about it.'

'Who said so?'

'Edwin Smith.'

'Who's he when he's at home?'

'A capitalist millionaire.'

She blew out her lips, but asked questions. He tried not to gloat, but she seemed impressed by this major shareholder in supermarkets and breweries, and only when she looked at the half-finished picture of Jo Feaver did her aggression reappear. Worth, with satisfaction, explained that Miss Feaver was a friend of Smith's.

'Did he commission it?'

'Yes.' He'd not heard a word from him, either.

'Well, make the sod pay. She's not exactly pretty, is she?'

'Never mind her,' he said. 'What about the work of art?'

'Has its points.'

'But no value in the class war?'

'You're getting ahead of yourself tonight,' she answered. 'If I wanted a political artwork you'd be the last man in the world I'd come to see. But you can paint. I'll give you that. You can paint.'

Pleased, he offered her gin. She refused, roughly demanding to see his sketches for the mural. She spent long enough over the last two skinhead pictures, surprisingly neglectful of his drawings of the riot damage.

'I think,' she said, 'I begin to see what you're getting at.' Her commentary played on the aesthetic not the political values of the works, and she spoke with skill about the balance, the effectiveness, the emotive power of his pencil lines. 'You're

124

somebody,' she concluded. 'I can't understand how anyone who acts so feebly as a man, can be so good on paper.'

'Perhaps that's the reason. I'm making up for my insecurities and inadequacies.'

'You're bloody lucky, then. I wish I could.' He waited for her, in the chill of the studio, the great sketchbooks open. 'I feel like death.'

'Do you mean you're ill?'

'Ill? Ill? What's that to do with it?'

He packed his drawings away and the pair drifted back to the dining room. While he washed the dishes, she sat making no attempt either to talk or to give him a hand, but when he returned she said suddenly, 'I've had a disappointment.'

Worth cleared the cloth, folded his table and waited for her confession. In the end, she fiddled deep in her handbag for some instrument and touching, playing with her cuticles, grumbled that she had quarrelled with Stuart Stout, who was a poseur, an ambitious, uncaring hypocrite. There followed a long, not uninteresting account of how Stout had ratted on his friends, let down a community association merely to curry favour from his party bosses. 'I wouldn't mind if . . . ' The words twanged off, over and again. He'd so often condemned 'politics is the art of the possible' in his colleagues, and now here he was, and the reason she could see plainly: personal advantage. When Worth, not entirely serious, suggested that Stout was at last learning sense, was trying to do something instead of carping at the efforts of the rest, she turned on him as the worst sort of cynic. 'Politics is people.' Her face reddened, and he examined the grammar of the sentence, coming down in her favour to her annoyance.

'You were fond of him,' he said.

'What's that mean?' Frowning.

'My spies report you've been seen walking hand in hand along the streets with Councillor Stout.'

'Who told you that?'

'You don't deny it,' he said gently, wishing he'd kept his mouth shut.

'I knew there was nothing for me on that score. He's married.'

'And a Catholic.'

She put away her instrument of manicure and with show of ill temper shook her handbag as if to restore chaos to its contents. They sat in silence, neither looking at the other.

'It's over and done with now, thank God.' Father's daughter.

'But the ideals you thought he stood for, don't they still count?'

'You stick to your painting.'

He expected her to flounce out, but she continued to sit, as if any company were better than her own. Ursula was not lively, and when she tried to win something of her own back by questioning him about Monica Pilgrim she could barely raise the appearance of malice. They drank gin, very little, talked desultorily and, when she refused a lift, walked back together through the coolish September streets.

'Your private detective will be making a report on this,' she said. She held his arm, not out of affection but as one who needed help along the way. As they turned down a side road where the orange lights lit the leaves of the lime trees, and great bunches and banks of shadow massed behind the roughly illuminated surfaces of front-garden walls she said he ought to paint like that.

'You also said you needed detail.'

Her voice had strengthened; he smelt her perfume, but when he put his lips to her mouth, she averted her face, politely eased him away. 'I'm shattered,' she said. 'I can't bear you to touch me.'

As she spoke, she clung to the arm of his anorak, a further beautiful complication in the half-dark.

They could see the lights still burning in her home, where her father had probably fallen asleep, she said, over the television. Neither of them knew what time the programmes closed down, and that seemed to him typical of his ignorance of the world of people, of feeling. He could make marks on paper, and there was his limit. Ursula did not hang about in the street, but disengaged herself, thanked him and marched smartly, independently up the garden path. After all, it was half-past midnight.

'Shall I see you again?' he called out.

'Christ knows,' she said, and went in.

14

By the end of September when the St Martin's summer gave way to rain and coldish nights, Worth had completed the portrait of Jo Feaver, and had begun to work on the sketches of Derbyshire under snow from earlier in the year. He tried to make the grey canvas part of the texture of the picture, using paint thinly, bleakly against the leafless black of the trees, the stone walls, the outcrops, the thinly snow-sprinkled grass. Unsure of himself, he forced his hands to work economically, parsimoniously with paint; these efforts reflected the chill of his spirits.

He inquired by telephone about Turnbull, but always meaning to call round, never managed it. He saw nothing of Ursula Quinn, except for a chance meeting in a supermarket when both gabbled that they were always busy, and at that minute in a tearing hurry. Worth wondered why he had said anything so foolish, had not detained the girl. Edwin Smith had not yet inspected or paid for the picture of Jo who reported him as in Manchester, Glasgow, Belfast and Oslo, but dying to see the results.

'How long,' Worth asked her, 'does it take to look at a painting?'

'How long is a piece of string?' she mocked. 'You don't know Smithy.'

'Go on.'

'He'd want to prepare himself. Take a day or two staring at me as if he were about to paint me himself. And then he'd ask me to describe your effort. So that he could imagine it; exact dimensions, colours, whether it was a good likeness, what I thought its strengths and weaknesses were. I'd also guess he'd like to quiz you in the same way if that were possible, to talk the thing off the canvas. That's why I keep coming to look, and make notes, so that I can answer his questions. Of course, it might be vanity. I could stare at it all day and every day.'

'Why does he do this?'

'To see if after all the description and his imaginative efforts and mine, you can surprise him. He won't just come once; he'll keep dodging in and out. That's why you haven't heard from him. He's not had time. He's really serious about art.'

He had written to the London gallery about his mural, but they had not deigned to reply. When he phoned, some choice secretary said Mr Albert was in Brussels, and Mr Victor still on holiday, but she would pass on his message. She knew nothing of Walden, gave the impression she'd never heard the name. Worth became suspicious, fearing that recession had sunk Burden Brothers, and that the principals had planted a stone-walling assistant in an empty office, while they fled their creditors. He tried a week later, talked to Victor Burden who was subdued, depressed and who, though encouraging him to collect work for another exhibition, would not put a provisional date on it, said he must consult his brother, who did the money end. 'Times are hard,' Burden said. 'There's no money about for art these days. Not even from people buying as investment. I have never known it so bad. But,' his voice lost nothing of its lugubrious polish, 'don't stop painting.'

Walden was in America, doing a little for the gallery, but mostly lecturing, at universities and museums. 'He really is an expert in modern art. World-renowned. You're very lucky you have such a man as an admirer.' That cheered Worth for all of an hour. Albert Burden had heard nothing of the mural, but believed the client, he clipped off eight or a dozen impressive Arab syllables, had not returned to England.

That evening Edwin Smith arrived in his Rolls Royce.

'What are you doing?' he asked. 'Am I interrupting anything?' It was past ten o'clock. 'You look like a late bird to me.'

They went together into the studio, where Smith ordered him not to put on any heat, because quizzing the portrait would not occupy much time. He stood in front of the painting, then donned spectacles, then snatched them off. Worth placed himself behind the man, so that he could see nothing of the facial expressions.

'Very good,' Smith pronounced, rather dully. He stalked round, bending to examine the back, before he said, 'Won't be dry yet?' He waddled to one side. 'Any sketches?' Worth produced them; Smith showed pleasure. 'What do I owe you?'

'What do you think?'

'Eleven hundred, with these three – ' he indicated the pencil sketches – 'thrown in.'

'Twelve.' Smith looked up, as if to argue.

'Agreed.' He scribbled the cheque. 'Have you finished touching this up?' He grinned at his expression. 'I'm looking forward to seeing it in daylight.'

'What does Jo think?'

'Likes it. Haven't had much time to talk to her. She's thinking of writing a monograph on you. Has a degree in fine art, so she'd know the words. Does that please you?'

'I don't know.'

'She must have been impressed. You're a marvellous draughtsman.' He scowled down at the portrait, wagged his fingers in a bunch. 'The colours are beautiful here. Restrained, but really something. We shall make a celebrity of you, John Worth.'

'Who's we?'

'I'll take the sketches.' He removed them, with care, himself. 'I'll collect this next time I'm home. We've just time for one drink in the nearest pub. Where is it?'

The night was chilly, starless; they walked the two minutes to the main road and the Three Crowns. Worth, cheque left lying on his studio table, felt dazed, incapable of coping with reality. He sipped his half of lager and listened to laughter. Smith, whisky, water and ice in a tumbler, special order, praised; nothing seemed usual. The massed bottles shone jewelled, seen through tears. Heroes stalked the floor; the bearded Viking behind the bar steered for new worlds. The two stayed for fifteen minutes and one drink; long shudders ploughed Worth's back as he watched Smith drive his Rolls away.

By nine next morning Worth was at work, again on a Derbyshire oil, this time of a clump of black trees and a hill.

It did not snow, but the sky was leaden, and the bleached grass danced.

The front door bell rang. He consulted his watch, and put brushes and palette carefully down, in the hope that the caller would disappear before he reached the door. 10.32.

A broad, handsome young man, with a fair drooping moustache, stared at him. 'Mr Worth?' He admitted it. 'Piers Turnbull.' The visitor shoved his hands deeply into the pockets of his anorak, as he stepped past the painter into the hall, where he wheeled, surprising his host. 'I've bad news.' He did not continue.

'Let's sit down, shall we?'

The man did not stir, blocking the passage with his breadth of shoulder.

'My father has died. Yesterday.'

'Uh. I see. I'm, uh, very sorry. Is . . . ?' He'd had enough.

'He committed suicide.'

Now it was out, Piers Turnbull saw fit to move, ungraciously.

In the kitchen the pair seated themselves at the table, the young man pulling at the neck of his shirt. Stomach cramped, Worth waited, not helpfully, examining the formica with eye and finger.

'How's Millicent taking it?' he asked, too late, in a clogged voice.

'Very well, really. She found him.'

'Where was he?'

'In bed. Whisky and sleeping tablets.'

Again they sat, not in antagonism, but in miserable ignorance of how to act, two men with much to say, unable to speak. Worth made an effort. He was the elder. 'How did it happen?'

'Millicent usually comes home for lunch on Thursdays, but this day she and a couple of other girls in the office had decided to go down to the pub for a drink and a snack. It was somebody's birthday. She'd arranged this some time before; my dad knew all about it. She'd cut him sandwiches, he was quite likely not to bother eating unless she left the food there right under his nose, and there was a casserole all ready in the

130

oven with instructions when to turn it on. Dad was quite a cook, you know, but these last months he wouldn't lift a finger.'

'What did he do all day?'

'Sat. Fiddled with the *Guardian*. Didn't turn the radio on. Might not even make himself a cup of tea. That's why she liked to come back at lunchtime. He'd rouse himself a bit while she was there. But the others wanted to go out yesterday, and dad had seemed so much better.'

'She isn't blaming herself, is she?' Worth asked.

'I wouldn't know that. She's not said as much.'

Once more the stupidity of silence divided them.

'What happened?' Worth's question hacked out like a phlegmy cough.

'She came in at about five-twenty, as usual, and couldn't smell the casserole, and thought he'd forgotten. She always left a list of duties pinned up for him in the kitchen.' For Turnbull, the efficient schoolmaster who'd chased scrimshankers, encouraged the falterers, who'd made it all work out. 'The door was locked, but this wasn't unusual because he knew she had a key. She called up; there was no answer. The oven wasn't on. He hadn't opened the tin where she'd put his sandwiches. There were no coffee cups on the draining board; he washed up very rarely. She ran upstairs, and he lay in bed. She thought he was asleep, she said; he seemed quite natural, head on one side. When she went right up to him, she saw he'd been slightly sick, but he was dead. The ambulance took him away.'

'Had he left a note?'

'Yes. To her. He asked forgiveness, and said she'd be better off without him.' Piers's eyes filled with tears, as if the horror had seized him.

Worth expressed sorrow, explaining how Turnbull had taken care of him when he was teaching, how well-organized his senior had been.

'He was nervous,' Piers said, 'all his life. He didn't look it; one tends to think of small, pale, twitching men. But he didn't sleep well, and would be up in the morning brewing tea. If we stayed out ten minutes longer than we said we would, he'd shake, not with anger, with anxiety. There was some desperate uncertainty in him.'

131

'Why was that?'

'His older brother did well. In the civil service. He's retired now with a knighthood. He was quite a bit older than dad, and the grandparents always compared them. They never had anything to do with each other, not even Christmas cards. He lives in Jersey.'

'Have you written?'

'Yes. Just a plain note. He'll find some excuse not to come.' Piers's face grew taut, with an anger which thinned his lips. 'I didn't mince words, and don't see why I should.'

'Yes.' This all seemed unnecessary. 'Is there anything I can do. Would it be any good if I came round to see Milly?'

'Yes, if you would. I've written to my mother and I expect she'll want to be at the funeral. She led him a pretty dance in her time.'

'I didn't know.'

'You don't appear to know much, Mr Worth.' The sentence shocked; Piers numbered him amongst the villains.

'Your father was very kind to me when I was going through a bad patch. I shall always be grateful. I wasn't much cop at teaching, but what bit I learned I learned from him. Perhaps I ought to have been more observant, but he seemed in charge, as nobody else was in that place.'

'My mother pushed him. To apply elsewhere for promotion.'

'He was capable.'

'He had a poor degree. He never got over that. If he'd won an international trial in rugby, I don't think it would have made up: not even a cap. He felt he was born to lose.'

'That's not how we saw him.'

'You didn't live at home with him.'

'I'm sorry.'

'He'd his faults. He harried Natalie. He wasn't satisfied till I got to Oxford where his big brother went. It wasn't comfortable, I can tell you. And then he married Millicent Tombs, threw my mother overboard. We never understood it, how it happened, where he found the courage. She was such a mouse, but she pushed him into it, must have done. He'd never have dumped my mother, otherwise. He depended too much on her.

132

And Natalie went for him, stood up for her mother, though she didn't get on with her, either. But Mill was four years younger than she was; she's younger than I am. That's what ruined Nat's marriage to Alan Ball, in so far as one can assign . . .' Piers broke off. 'It was a bloody mess then, and it's a bloody mess now.'

'What will Milly do?'

'Do?'

'Will she go on living there? In the place? Will it belong to her?'

'About all that will. My mother took her share, and more. All his savings went so that he could keep the house. He'd nothing; he's still shelling out. That's what he called it. Christ.'

Worth fetched down the whisky bottle, poured slugs, turned the conversation to Piers's progress at Oxford. He'd almost finished writing up his D.Phil; there were one or two bits needing attention before the final typing, but it was in the bag, he thought, unless some nutter was put on to examine it. And after that? He shrugged his shoulders, the broad shoulders he'd inherited from his father, and grimaced. There would be nothing for him at Oxford, or anywhere else. He was too well qualified for a schoolmaster; they wanted mediocrities, and besides. 'You can see what that did for Dad,' he said, teeth clenched. 'First-class honours, doctorate; unemployable. The finest product of the system he'd worked for, and unwanted.'

They had an hour together and Worth liked the young man, who was clever and politely forceful, but gave nothing away about his father's death.

When, on the next evening, Worth called at the Turnbulls' house, he was shown in by Natalie Ball, dressed in her street clothes, announcing to him that she had to be on her way. She introduced him into the kitchen where after a few minutes of chit-chat, she buttoned her coat, wished Piers and Millicent goodbye, grasped Milly by the elbow, said, 'I shall pray for you,' and left, a dark, Spanish-looking woman, with beautiful, ringless hands. Neither of the younger people commented.

Millicent flapped flour-covered arms helplessly towards the visitor, indicating that she could not shake hands. She was

133

rolling out, cutting pastry to cover three meat pies. She shaved long slivers from the edge of the plates, to make decorative leaves for the centre of the crust, rolled the spare into a lump and said that as a child she sweetened this, added currant eyes and shaped it into a rhino. They laughed, subdued and polite. Piers, sleeves tucked back, began to wash the utensils crowding the sink; Worth reached for a teatowel; nobody mentioned Turnbull as they talked about cookery. The scene was domestic; Piers and Milly might have been a young married couple; she seemed mildly excited, and when she had cleared up, volleyed instructions, she shot out of the room. The two men immediately ceased talking, worked side by side. Worth broke the silence to mumble that he would not put cutlery away and ruin the system. Piers did not answer.

They had almost finished when Millicent returned. She had removed her pinafore, changed her dress, spent some time on her hair. Talk burst out as she stacked the dishes, once ordering Piers to re-wash a plate. Worth wondered when, and how, he should introduce the subject of Turnbull's suicide; the others seemed in no hurry. They moved to the dining room, sat in front of a discoloured gas fire.

'Do you know?' Millicent began, ended.

'Yes?' Worth.

'I shall never be able to decorate that front room now.'

'Why not?'

'I shall have to sell the place. Piers and I have talked about it.'

'Wouldn't it add to the value of the house if you smartened it?' Worth.

She turned towards the younger man.

'I'd never thought of that.' She brushed her finger ends across her forehead. 'I don't really think Teddy wanted me to do it. We never went in there. It smells of damp. I think it was a sort of taboo. If I interfered, something awful would happen.'

Perhaps she suddenly grasped what she had said, and a silence chilled the room. Worth understood the irrational fears that had haunted Turnbull, the everyday terrors this girl had grappled with.

'I kept saying,' she had begun again, voice bright as a

134

blazer button, 'that if I didn't do it, you wouldn't sell your mural to the Arab sheik. It was superstitious, and yet I believed it. I think Teddy wanted you to paint that, he thought it might make your name; but he kept dissuading me, or delaying. He could easily have cleared his rubbish out since he's not been at school.'

'We can't always bring ourselves to do what we want,' Worth said.

'That's true.' She had cried in his presence when her husband had seemed to be recovering, and now talked steadily as a garrulous shopkeeper. 'I keep going to work. It's the most sensible thing. Piers has been very good.'

'I'm very sorry about Ted. He was a good friend to me.' He'd come out with it, at last, and awkwardly enough. It had to be said; she had to hear, and hear again, and learn to bear it. He made a few remarks about his own incapacity as a schoolmaster, about Turnbull's skill, devotion, interest. Such work must have taken its toll. They listened with suitably sober faces, saying nothing, so that he developed his theme, stumblingly: in the schools such men as Teddy Turnbull had a great, unappreciated effect on pupils and colleagues and thus on the generations to come. Never was so much owed by so many to so few. Nor did the education service itself recognize this solid merit; its officers fostered the glib, the specious, the meretricious, the personally ambitious. The two young people sat side by side, slightly puzzled, faces frozen into seriousness, Piers leaning away from Millicent, with one elbow on the table. Worth, bemused with his own loquacity, wondered if he was anywhere near the truth, but continued to expatiate, not displeased with himself.

When he stopped, the children – they looked so to his thirty-two years – nodded.

'Would you like,' Millicent said, 'to go and see him?'

'See?'

'At the chapel of rest. He's at the hospital now for the postmortem before the inquest, but when they've done, he'll be . . . We had to go to the mortuary for formal identification this morning. It was quick; they were really nice. But when he's laid

135

out, perhaps . . .' Even then her voice did not falter, she merely chose not to choose words.

'Well, I . . .' He floundered.

'Let us know.' Piers, matter-of-fact.

'You're a painter,' she said. 'You must look for experience.'

It hit him as incredible that two days after her husband's suicide she was inviting him to make artistic capital from the death; human beings transcended accepted clichés. He did not relish it; she should have acted otherwise.

'I'd like to go,' he answered.

He stayed another half-hour and though Millicent described the finding of her husband's body, Piers held her hand, it became clear that both were beginning to regard Turnbull's self-destruction as a natural death, unpleasant, shocking, but bearable. They could come to terms with it. They led him to the front gate, thanking him effusively; they would let him know the date of the funeral.

On his way home he turned, unusually, into the pub where he and Smith had celebrated their bargain. A saturnine young man behind the bar served him with a whisky mac, saying it was a bit parky now in the evenings. The bar shone; light from bottles, from polished wood surfaces, chrome, copper gleamed but could be doused by a finger on a switch. Muzak spurted from its cassette. Nor were there many clients, and the few stood subdued, propping themselves up. The one centre of life sounded in the far corner where a young man bent over the one-armed bandits, shoving in money, carefully feathering his controls.

'Give us another quid's worth of ten *p*s, Ken,' he said, not looking up. He completed his operation and approached the bar holding out a pound note.

'Are you winnin'?' a bystander asked.

'What d'you think?'

All returned to their absorbed concerns, and nobody wished him goodnight.

Worth met Piers by chance in the street, and he reported that the inquest had been painless, under a considerate coroner. The funeral service at St Michael's was well attended, three rows of schoolchildren and staff, ex-rugby and cricket players in black ties, with white shirts, Edgar Quinn in a suit with a trilby.

'I thought I'd pay my last respects.' Quinn buttonholed Worth outside the church as they waited for the cortege to draw away. 'A tragedy. He's a man I'd always admired. Never knew when he was beat on the rugby field.'

'How did you come to have an interest in rugby?'

'Through a pal of mine. Lived next door. He won a scholarship and played at the high school, an' I used to go as a lad and watch him. And then we biked it down to the county ground for the 'ome games. Long after I was married. And "Topsy" Turnbull, he was one of the stars, then. Young chap. Not long out of Leeds University.' Worth had not heard the sobriquet before, debated if it were private between Quinn and his companion. 'Beautiful player. Wing forward. Kept that pack going. Did six men's work. Of course, he was very strong, and fast with it. Tragedy. Do they know why he did it?'

'Depression.'

'Wouldn't be as old as me. Powerful man. Don't seem right. It only seems five minutes since; ordering 'em in the line-out. Young. Fierce chap. But a gentleman. None of this fist and boot you get on the telly, even in internationals. It's a bastard.'

Quinn had rarely shown such animation or concern outside himself. Had this dissatisfied grumbler carried over from his young manhood a hero worship that was untarnished by the malice, the gall of the older self? Or was it a performance?

'The wife looked very young and pale, I thought.' Quinn straightened the set of his hat. 'She was his second. You know 'em, though. I remember his first. Used to see her down at Beeston. Beautiful, dark woman, high colour, hair in those ear-phone coils. Always dressed in bright colours, reds, y'know. Striking.'

'She was here today.'

'Was she? I didn't see her.'

'She sat with the family. Her hair's grey.'

'It would be, wouldn't it?'

Quinn answered Worth's questions about Ursula unwilling-ly, whining that she was never at home, spent her time at

137

political meetings or pushing revolutionary pamphlets through the doors of illiterate blacks, or blethering about Trotsky to half a dozen others as crackbrained as she was.

'I say to her, "What the 'ell do you know about poverty? You was brought up on the fat of the land. Me and your mother sacrificed to give you an education. And what's the result? You go trampin' the bleddy streets encouraging these louts and lootin' yobboes to riot, to holl bricks through shop windows. You're off your head," I say to her. "Off your bloody lunatic 'ead." '

'And she?'

'Usual. I'm conditioned by the capitalist press, wage-slave mentality. All the rest of the clap-trap. I tell her straight, "Bloody 'ooligans," I say, "they should shove 'em in the army like I had to." Wouldn't do her any harm, neither.' Quinn's foxy eyes narrowed. 'Will she lose her job, d'you think, if she goes on like this?'

'Doubtful. As long as she keeps it out of school.'

'But will she?'

Quinn returned to his hero. That was the man; children could learn from his likes. He described a tackle on some huge international in full flight. 'Run with his knees right high, this fellow, kneecaps up to his chin. An' fourteen ston' if he were a pound. But Topsy upended him and he hit the ground like a ton of 'oss muck. Couldn't breathe, couldn't see, couldn't walk. That bleddy internationalled him.'

By the time they reached the Quinns' house, Edgar had talked himself out, and hunched his way across the pavement, barely capable of mouthing thanks for the lift. Worth wasted half an hour at home washing his hands or rustling the newspaper before he made his way to the Turnbulls'. The cremation service had been for family only, but a few friends were invited back to the house.

The atmosphere was cheerful, unsubdued; people called out, moved round easily, rattled down their cups and plates, laughed. One saw little formal mourning; only the headmaster and two other middle-aged men wore black ties; Piers had a neck-high sweater, in brown. Millicent came over immediately

138

to Worth, thanked him for coming, for wreath and message, and led him to the dining-room table where a bosomy lady, unknown to him, handed out strong tea and indicated the choice of sandwiches. The noise doubled. He was reminded of the single Sunday School treat he had attended, held indoors because of rain, where many bosses disorganized the existing small chaos.

Elspeth Turnbull confronted him, introducing herself. 'I don't know whether I'm welcome here,' she said, 'but they invited me.' She looked older than her years, the outline of her chin broken, the forehead scored, the grey hair untidy, greasy. There was no flamboyance of dress today; a rather old-fashioned two-piece, with blouse, cameo brooch; one could not quite smell the camphor balls.

Worth made conventional remarks about the death, Turnbull's kindness to him, even quoted Quinn, on the tackle, on her appearances on the touchline.

'I wonder how many of us will be remembered vividly like that in twenty-five years,' he said.

'You've got your painting. The pictures will be there after you've gone.'

'They'll be seen. People won't need to remember. I'll be condemned off my own brush.'

'Oh,' she said, nostrils widening. 'That friend of yours remembered him properly. He was a very good player. Very good indeed. There's no doubt if he'd played for one of the London clubs he'd have won an international cap.'

Worth, abashed, muttered something about tragedy, but that didn't suit, either.

'I don't want to make a thing of it,' her appearance belied the words, 'but probably this was the best course he could have taken. He'd passed his peak, years back.' She did not lower her voice; he shrank inside his suit. 'Downhill all the way.'

He objected; Turnbull was highly thought of at his school.

'There are hundreds of respected teachers,' she said. 'I'm one of them. But as a young man he was outstanding. And he knew when his day was over. I made better progress on the educational ladder than he did, in spite of my breaks for the

139

children. No, he knew he was a run-of-the-mill teacher, and couldn't come to terms with it. He knew, too, that he hadn't made enough of his talent as a rugger player; he should have pushed himself into the places where the selectors were. He knew it. Perhaps he didn't care at the time, but he bitterly regretted it when it was too late. He could have played for England, and he didn't.' She sounded angry herself; wrinkles deepened, dirtied. 'That's why he turned odd. Lost his head over this girl.' Worth glanced about; nobody listened, approached, bothered. 'Not that I'm complaining. It was the best thing that could have happened to me. I dropped into a better job than I'd have got here, and at the right time, just before they started the squeeze on schools. But, no. He couldn't come to terms with what he was. And I presume he grew worse and worse.'

'Well, I don't know . . .'

'Nobody knows. Millicent's nice enough. A little innocent, I expect. And sly, I shouldn't be surprised. But she couldn't know what she was taking on. How could she? Natalie's marriage wasn't what he wanted, and now that's cracked up. Piers is clever, has done well, but he's getting nowhere fast, just like his father; history repeating itself.'

'None of us likes getting old.'

'I don't mind. And he wasn't old at fifty.'

She deserted him, carried on an energetic conversation with her daughter. Worth listened to the headmaster of Turnbull's school laying down the law about what he called the 'Protestant work ethic'. A red-faced man made some remarks to him, almost surrealistically, about golf. Piers thanked him, said he'd be staying for a week or two until Millicent made up her mind. 'I feel some responsibility for her.'

'Does she not have anything to do with her parents?'

'Not really. They'll write or phone for a birthday.'

'Don't they get on?'

'I've no idea. She hardly mentions them.'

'Do they know about, about your father's death?'

'Yes. She wrote, and had a polite note back. It made the sort of noises I expected. But they were preparing to fly out to Malta to stay with friends, and there was no thought of putting that off.' Piers looked about for Milly, saw her by the window, composed, plate in hand. 'She'll be right enough. She has a good job, you know, really responsible. I was surprised.'

As Worth left he noticed that the door of the drawing room was closed.

15

While John Worth struggled to come to terms with Turnbull's death, he suddenly heard good news from the Burden Galleries. Two of his pictures had been sold, very profitably, to an American who wanted to see more, and who would buy sketches. Instructions were given as to what he was to send up for framing. Victor advised him to act at once and ascribed this breakthrough to Walden who had 'been preaching his gospel in the States'. Second, after a protracted negotiation, one of the Sunday colour supplements had chosen to make a print from his *Winter Wood*, one of this Burwell Park paintings. 'I had a bit of a struggle with their art people,' Victor wrote, 'but it will sell. The print's made, and is beautiful. You'll turn a nice sum out of that.' He roughly indicated the time when Worth would be asked to come up to London for the signing chore. 'Let's hope the weather's not too bad, and then we'll make a fuss of you.' Third, he'd secured Worth a commission for record sleeves. 'You'll do this on your head, you'll enjoy it; you'll get publicity out of it. You're about to become well known, young man.'

In all this wealth of gladness there was, typically, no mention of the Arab mural.

Josephine Feaver wrote him a letter, very formal in language, asking him for an interview because Edwin Smith had pressed her to begin the monograph on Worth's painting. He telephoned her three times before he found her in, and she

141

proposed to appear that evening since she had her preliminary questions ready. When she arrived she was wearing scruffy jeans, a Trent Polytechnic t-shirt under a huge, fur-collared anorak, but she carried a clipboard, a selection of biros. She refused offers of refreshment.

'No,' she said, 'let's sit down and get on with it. I'm on edge. We'll make friends a bit later.'

He was amused by her businesslike speed. What photographs of pictures existed? What pictures were where. She named three she would like to trace. She scribbled addresses, and commented that this was the side of the work she liked least. 'People are so variable. Some never reply. Others inundate you with information you don't want or pile work on you with their idiocies. Yes, she had written monographs and introductions to catalogues: Paul Nash, Egon Schiele, Pollock, R.B. Kitaj, Art Déco, Erotic Painting in Pre-war Germany. She knew gallery directors, had worked with Roy Strong. 'They like me because I'm careful, have no axes to grind, will take their advice and can defend myself. The fact that I'm no longer in the trade is a great advantage.'

'How old are you?' he asked, out of the blue.

'Thirty-eight.' Unembarrassed.

'You don't look twenty-eight.'

She pulled a sour face, tapped her board. 'I shall have to ask you about yourself,' she said.

'And draw conclusions?'

'I'm a pragmatist. I'm interested in your work. I shall say some things that will annoy you, but you'll have the chance to discuss them with me, and convince me I'm wrong. But it's not likely that I shall claim you paint the way you do because your mother was frightened by a passing motor-bike on the night you were conceived. Grant me at least a modicum of common sense, will you? Now, start to talk.'

She switched on a recorder.

Worth found it difficult to dredge up energy to formulate the principles behind his painting, the motives, the first inclinations.

'I don't know why I paint. It's what I wanted to do from a lad

142

when I was at the grammar school, though the headmaster there wasn't keen. After that, it's what I was trained for. I'm compulsive, I suppose, because I feel guilty if I'm not doing something about it, but I take it that's habit. Nor do I much like talking about it. I don't really understand what's going on, it's half unconscious or subconscious, and I don't think I want to know.'

'That's good,' she praised. 'You're very articulate.'

'There are too many *I*s in it for my liking.'

She did not press him, but led him to remember his parents, both now dead. They had bought this house when he was in the third year of grammar school; both had worked at the time, his father as manager of a large furniture store, his mother as a school secretary. They were determined to give him all he needed, and more.

'Were they in any way artistic?'

'I'd say so. My father was very good with a pencil, and so was my grandfather, or so I'm told. They were both untrained. Never even attended night-school classes. And my mother could embroider, and sew, and knit marvellously, neatly and like lightning. She made her own patterns up.' He fetched over a large cushion; the design showed hills sweeping down to a lake, great tumbles of cloud, vivid in still bright colours, but with a broad simplicity of mass.

'It's great,' Jo said. 'None of your concern with detail. Perhaps it's the medium.'

He dashed out into the other room, returning with a second cushion, this time embroidered with an abstract design, in blacks, whites, ruby reds, stone colours, a kind of crazy checker-board, with the small squares edged out of shape, a stagger of harmonious colour and zigzag pattern.

'That really is satisfying,' Jo said. 'I wonder if she saw the whole design before she started, or modified it as she progressed.'

'You'd never get her to say anything about it. Something to be done, not discussed.'

'Like mother, like son.'

They laughed, pleased with each other.

143

'They'd no idea what was required of me. I don't think they really wanted me to study art. The lad I biked to school with did sciences and became a dental surgeon. That was a good career. But once I'd made my mind up, they supported me as well as kept out of my way. I wasn't pleasant to them at that time. I had to fight my way against grammar school advice, and I wasn't sure. I always did well at lessons, but it wasn't until I got up to London and began winning prizes there that they thought I might be on the right track. Oh, they were delighted when they saw my schoolboy stuff on exhibition at the Castle, but they were fundamentally insecure, needed signposts and pats on the shoulder and friendly schoolmasters or newspapers or bosses to tell them they were doing well.'

'Don't we all?' she said.

'Well, now. That's right, and it puts pressure on us to prove something about ourselves. And I suppose if nobody bought our pictures, or looked at them, or said a word in our favour, we'd lose heart in the end. I think I would. But I tell you this, even when I'm struggling and wondering whether or not I'm wasting my time and everybody else's on a project, at bottom I've confidence I'm doing the right thing, am in the right part of the globe.'

'To this end I was born,' she quoted solemnly. 'Did you get good teachers?'

'So-so. I think I profited most from the fuddy-duddies, the "you learn to draw as well as Raphael and then you can make up your mind what sort of fancy-work you choose for yourself" school.'

'And that's right, you think?'

'It was for me. I liked, did well at, these academic exercises. Streets of buildings and plaster casts of Socrates.'

'And life classes?'

'Yes. I was too fluent, if anything, found it too easy to knock off a sketch in the style of this master or that. One's tempted.'

'And your teachers? Didn't you admire their work?'

'Some. One, especially, Alf Gearing. But he wasn't much good at teaching because he wasn't much good at words. "Yes, yer," he'd say. "I don't see it like that. I suppose you could. If

144

you wanted to." I once asked him, "How do you see it, then?" and he made a bit of a drawing in the corner of my paper. Then he said, "That's not so good as yours, Worth." '

'And was it?'

'No, I don't think it was. He'd no interest in what we were doing, a male nude, if I remember. But I was as pleased as punch because he'd remembered my name. He's dead now.'

'I've never seen anything of his. I've heard his name.'

'He died in his forties, and he wasn't prolific. He could paint. But it's the other students, especially at the Royal College, you learn from. There were some gifted people there in my time. There was one Australian boy, his paint fairly blazed off the paper. I'm no colourist, but he was wonderful, seared your eyeballs.'

'What's happened to him?'

'No idea. He went into advertising, I think. I've not noticed any of his pictures.'

'Why's that?'

'He may have gone abroad again. Oh, I see what you mean. Talent's not enough. This may sound excessive, especially as I seem to be applying it to myself, but it's demon, spirit, driving you headlong, forcing you to practise.'

'Ambition?' she asked.

He rubbed his chin.

'That may be another name for it. But it's ambition applied to paint and pencil. I may want to make money, or impress pundits or attract women into my bed, or I may think that's what I want, but it's the personality which makes me apply myself absolutely to work.'

'You believe in yourself?' she asked.

'I wish I knew.'

Jo Feaver looked over his albums, his notebooks, his pictures, and sent a photographer in. She was not a nuisance, acted as a goad, with suggestions for development, pulled his leg, made him laugh. He looked forward to her visits, painted all day, sketched her for another portrait.

'You're a marvel,' he said one evening as she, about to leave, stood in the passage. Jo put out a hand and stroked his chest, in a gesture both loving and neutral.

'Don't go getting fond of me, young fellow,' she warned, laughing before she kissed him, then pushed him roughly back.

Victor Burden telephoned to say he'd be in the city, visiting his daughter, Lady Humphreys, and would call to see what he was up to. The dealer silently inspected canvas and paper, a bald, bird-eyed, hook-nosed individual, who looked from a picture to his fingernails and back, and then silently indicated that Worth should turn on.

'Yes,' he said, at the finish, 'yes.' He sat down at the kitchen table, untroubled, chin in hand, as Worth bustled about with coffee in his mother's best china. What he was about was impossible to guess; he perched impassive, immovable, sallow, not formidable, but self-contained. The painter darted about, putting off the interview, a raw shudder scoring the craven flesh of his back, afraid of the verdict. In the end Victor Burden flagged him down into a chair; that seemed a miniature victory.

'Worth,' Burden said, 'you've changed.' Did he want an answer? He did not get it. 'Sometimes for the better, sometimes not. Can you account for it?'

'Not offhand.'

'That's right. It's not your business to explain. You've been working, though. By God, you have.' He hummed, a Mozartian snatch. 'You've never been an idler, but this last few months you've stepped up production. I've a little slot, February–March. That's why I came in. We'll put an exhibition up. We'll have to hurry, and it's not an ideal time. But we'll do it. After I'd seen this performance tonight I wondered whether to put it off, start to think big, but no. Those snow things of yours I'd sell tomorrow to America.'

The man talked, unemphatically, made one demand. 'I want a large, ten feet by six, centrepiece made of your *Christ's Entry into Jerusalem Three.*'

'You may not like it.'

'What's that to the point?' Burden cracked his knuckles. 'We think highly of you. That's why I bothered to call in to see if you'd done enough for an exhibition. You have, and more. I also think, maybe wrongly, that I can sell your stuff. I don't like it all, but why should I? I'll tell you what I like, and what I

146

don't, and why, if you really want to know, but what in hell does it matter? You get on as you are doing, and when I think you're producing what I can't sell I'll let you hear soon enough.'

Worth knew elation, but kept his face straight.

Walden, Victor Burden said, had been back from America some time, but was now in France. They'd heard nothing of the mural, but still. 'Georgie Walden admires you, and he's a friend to have, with marvellous contacts. If he says so, you're in, and you're in with powerful people.' Walden was Hungarian, not Jewish, his name originally György Kertész, but his part of the family had taken their name from the town in Essex. His brother became Curtis. Nobody knew how old he was, but he'd lived in England since the nineteen-twenties. 'One of these days somebody will write a book about him, and it'll make your hair stand on end. Been connected with art-dealing all his life, as his father and grandfather were, but he served in the Middle East during the war. DSO. The lot. We were glad to get him, my God. And he praises you.'

'Why?'

'I often ask myself that. With his background you'd expect he'd be attracted to something spicier. Goulash. Pörkölt. I'll press him sometimes, but he shrugs it off. "What use is talking?" he'll say. "You and I are interested in making money, not pontificating about art." He's bought three of your pictures, you know.'

Burden left, as always, precise instructions and dates, insisted on writing them down. When Worth mentioned Josephine Feaver's projected monograph, he took her name. 'Never heard of her, but we'll perhaps be able to use her.' He shook hands genially. 'Get that big thing up and started,' he said. 'We don't want thinking. Painting!'

By the next morning Worth had decided he'd paint on wood, and had then consulted timber merchants, knocking together a stand to hold the piece during the painting. This carpentry occupied a whole day and excited him. As soon as the board was delivered he'd prime it, and then would make the decisions. Procrastination seethed with importance; he looked over his sketches, but he allowed himself to do no more until the space,

147

the white ground tempted him. Now he felt it in the prickle of forearms, across the shoulders, in the movement of his bowels; his breath seemed held for him.

That evening he telephoned Millicent Turnbull who asked him round.

The girl looked bright, ordinary, in an overall, a smudge of dust by her mouth. She had started to clean the place up in preparation for a visit to the house agents. Piers and Natalie had been useless; at first Piers had helped, been a comfort, laughed with her, but was hopeless practically; they would not make up their minds for her.

'I'm a thrower-out,' she said. 'I have a bonfire every night, but I want them to have the things which remind them of their father. But they hesitate, and waste my time; they'll drive me cracked. I want to get on with it. I haven't the money to pay the rates and bills for a house this size for evermore.'

'You've given them the chance. They can't complain. And if they do, it can't affect you for much longer.'

'There might be quite a long period before I get the house off my hands.'

'Possible. Listen, I've a spare bedroom where you could store some of your . . .'

'Thanks. Do you think I should contact Elspeth to see if there's . . . She's quick at making her mind up, isn't she?'

'Mightn't she do something you don't like, take something you want? I mean, I don't know her, really.'

'I'll risk it.' She sounded brave enough, so that he suggested that they walk out for a drink, but she refused. 'No, just sit down there for half an hour and tell me all about yourself. Then I shan't think I'm deserted. I can cope, you know. I'm not a colonel's daughter for nothing.'

As he talked about the February exhibition, at first fluently, glad he'd much to say, he watched her pinched face. Here everything went right for him; for her nothing but retrenchment, withdrawal.

'I think you'll be famous,' she said, with spirit. 'How do you like the idea?'

'It appeals. But only so long as it doesn't prevent me from working.' Pompous.

148

'Is that likely?'

'Oh, yes. Half the thing about art is that it's irrational, hidden, so that you don't know what you're about; you're always struggling to find out for yourself. If you become well known, then there's publicity, and people tell you what you've done, or should do; it brings it all to the top of your head.'

'You shouldn't use your intelligence, then?'

'Of course. But it's not the be-all and end-all. I'd guess, anyway, the best situation is when you're on the way to recognition; not there, but not discouraged.'

'Better to travel hopefully . . . ?' she said.

He pulled a face at her.

'This is all about me,' he said.

'But that's because it's good. I want to talk about something cheerful.' She opened her eyes wide, laid small hands on the table. 'Nothing's going well for me. I feel so tired.'

'It will improve.'

'Time the great healer.' Her voice sounded more speculative than ironical.

'You're young,' he pressed.

'Doesn't that make it worse? Isn't that a stage when I can be really crippled for the rest of my life? I could see that people didn't understand why I should marry anyone as old as Teddy. Piers didn't. My parents didn't. But I wanted to. I loved him, and admired him and was flattered when he said he wanted to leave Elspeth and live with me. I didn't expect him to die. He seemed young, himself, and well organized, and if I was in trouble, he'd help me find out what to do. And at the same time he depended on me, for love, and comfort, and sex, and hope, he said. We quarrelled sometimes. He didn't always approve of what I did; my clothes for instance or how I spent my spare time. He wanted me to study, I think; he loved people learning from books. But I wanted to make the house pretty and serve him delicious meals.'

'Didn't he want that?'

'He liked being made a fuss of. You all do. Elspeth had been too busy getting on in her career lately. That was half the trouble. But he was a bit of an old puritan. He thought people should be busy improving their minds. It would have stuck six inches on his chest measurement to talk about Doctor Piers Turnbull.'

'I see.'

'Don't get me wrong. We were making something of it. I was lucky in that I'd found an interesting job. He'd got his school, and the rugby team, and the WEA class on local history he taught. We'd paid Elspeth off. We were starting to find our feet. We understood each other. We loved each other.'

Again her eyes opened largely, as if she tried to let in light on a mystery. Her face seemed set, a mask against the implacable enemy.

'It went wrong,' she said, at length, with a stony clarity.

'Do you want to talk about it?' he mumbled. 'There's no need. I don't want you needlessly upsetting yourself.'

She stared over at him, in a challenge, despising him, dismissing his charity.

'There was this basic insecurity in him,' she said. 'I didn't see it. Not at first. Here I was snivelling, throwing up my law course, staggering about like the damned. And there he was. Rock steady. A big teddy bear. Everybody's friend and strength and stay. A daddy who did really involve himself. It was only after we were married that I saw how much he lived on his nerves, and how little stamina, reserve, he really had. It was frightening. The signs were always there, I imagine, but I'd been in too much of an emotional mess myself to see them. So that when he cracked up . . .' Her voice tailed off as she raised her head; her white throat stretched vulnerable. 'It was awful at first. I'd never seen a man like that, in that state. Sometimes he was like a child who'd been thrashed. Or run over. And I had to have time off from work, and chase home in the lunch hour, and belt round chemists' shops and this place and that. But I could cope. I could really. And it made me feel pleased. I was often worn out, too tired to sleep sometimes, but I did think I could manage, especially when he seemed to be improving.' Her hands reached out, for nothing. 'When he had to go into hospital again, that was a setback, but then again I told myself it was all to the good, that he was in the best place. I got used to it.

150

Life seemed possible. When he came out he did have bad days, and they were awful, but it wasn't every day, and I'd delude myself that he'd recover, or so it seems now. And then he killed himself.' Her face turned white, a ghastly lifeless pallor as if the spoken sentence had cut off her blood. As she sat she seemed weightless, to be toppled by a puff of draught; only her head moved in a mechanical, small idiocy of swaying. She did not cry; nothing as comforting as tears remained to her.

When she tried to speak, she made small croakings.

He dared not go towards her. So they sat, she in grief, he incapable of gesture, and it was the woman who recovered first.

'It makes you wonder what's coming next,' she said.

'Yes.'

'You think it can't get worse. But it can. It can. I'm on the lookout for what will hit me next. They'll find I've got cancer or incurable kidney disease.'

'You don't feel ill, er, unwell . . . ?'

'Not in the way you mean. But that is how it would be. No warning signals. Fit as a fiddle one week; next, breasts cut off.'

'You're young,' he objected, feebly.

'That's what Teddy used to say. We were going along Valley Road in the car only in the summer, when he suddenly said to me, in a very glum way, as we passed the tennis courts, "I shall never play there again, not in my life." He was very good when he was younger, you know. I said, "Let's stop now and have a knock-up," but he didn't hear, or want to. I would probably use the courts sometime, and he wouldn't, and it seemed to him a matter of intense sadness.' She shook her head. 'Some days I don't feel too bad and I think I'm recovering, and then, without warning, it all drops on me, and down I slump.'

She poured a half-cup of coffee for herself.

'You do me good. You're there, and you're achieving something.'

'That's not how it seems to me,' he said.

'But it is so. You've your pictures. People can look at them, and admire them. I never saw Teddy when he was a great rugby player.'

'Old Quinn, Ursula's father, often talks about it.'

151

'That's all there is left. Some old chap. I used to hate daddy going on about India and the war and all the rest of it. You'll keep coming to see me, won't you? I don't know too many people here. And you're alive.'

That seemed meaningless. They talked a little longer, and as they did so she slipped away from him, into her sorrow.

'You'll come and visit me, won't you?' he asked, in the hall. She immediately began to question him again about the large *Entry of Christ*, and he explained how he'd set it up, how he'd decide where to start. She questioned him, appeared excited, steadier. Impulsively, she opened the drawing-room door, switched the light on to the dinginess of the room, the faded, frayed carpet, the discoloured wallpaper, the shabby humps of furniture, the piles of books about the untidy floor, the dust.

'Should I decorate that?' she asked.

'Why not?'

'I'll have to move his books, and his papers. There's all this local history. I don't know whether it's worth anything or not. I'll have to ask Professor Woodward. But your picture, it counts, doesn't it?'

'Counts?'

'I said I'd do this when you started your mural. This is as good, isn't it?'

'Don't you overdo things,' he ordered.

'I know exactly what colours I'll use. Exactly. I've been thinking about it long enough. I don't think he wanted me to do it, really. But it'll put value on the house, won't it?'

She led him inside to show him the fireplace tiles, and the marbled slate mantelpiece.

'They're good,' she announced. 'This could be a beautiful room. When are you going to start?'

'When they deliver my wood, and I find out whether or not this timber stand of mine will hold it up. It's quite a big affair. Looks like a siege engine.'

Her face fell again; the thin lips trembled. In the room cold damp oozed in the air. She switched off the light, pulling the door to. Her hands, as he shook them, were icy, and she stood so uncertainly, hair lifeless, that he thought she might topple as

152

soon as he had closed the front door behind him. He stood for a minute, half expecting a scream, a thud of collapse, but he could make nothing out through the stained glass, windmill and milk-blind clouds. She did not move to drop the catch, push the bolt. His ankle turned as he walked away, but he swore in relief, recovering balance.

16

The lorry with Worth's wood and supporting lengths banged up first thing in the morning, and he spent a further two days strengthening the piece, making certain that it stood securely. This period of carpentry elated him because it meant that his mind could play on the space without having to make a mark; frightened, he allowed his imagination free rein, and knocked off postcard-size sketches of the correct shape just to convince himself that he employed himself properly. If he hadn't to prepare the base, he would have been conscience-bound to begin the painting and he was not ready. This steady, art-school minion, this careful recorder of trees, knots, branches and leaves needed his unconscious to stagger, in daylight and in sleep, to drool the pattern in his mind that the skilled hand would detail into a picture.

So hammer and screwdriver gave him time, and he hummed and whistled about his studio, sure now that his picture would not warp, would remain heavy and solid, whatever his paintwork. When he had primed it, white, for he knew Christ must enter in the spring, in the light, in the brightness, in the juvenescence of the year, he marched up and down in front of the surface, touching it, tempting it to tempt him. He gave it a second and third coat and as he plied the wide brush he decided that he would begin work on Saturday. The rest of this day, and Friday, he would make himself sketch, take his decisions. He hung the studio with his earlier drawings, enjoying them, drawing no comfort from them for too often they seemed finished entities needing no completion elsewhere. The most articulate of his teachers at the RCA, a pedant, screwing his mouth, had instructed his students sourly, 'When you've decided the subject of your great masterpiece, just oblige me by making up your mind the country it takes place in, the time of year, the time of day and the weather. I don't see why that should obstruct the burgeoning imagination.' Worth searched out some of his spring drawing books, his photographs of skies, his annotated cloud sketches. Now terrified, he went off for an autumn walk.

As he stalked along, his eye snatched at detail: gorse bushes, a twisted silver birch, brambles, the late, bedraggled roses in gardens, the play of light on raw, suburban brickwork, the overalls of house painters on ladders, the rattle of a lorry allied to its mud-streaking colours, privet hedges, sodden paper, the immense and daunting complexity of a spray picked up from the gutter and twirled by its stalk.

He returned in a scutter of rain, cut hunks of bread and jam, Ursula's making; he had not eaten a cooked meal for four days, and having cleared his dining-room table leafed through sketches unconnected with the picture.

The telephone interrupted him. Walden's soft voice demanded to know if he could call in first thing in the morning.

'What time's first thing?' he heard himself asking.

'No later than ten.' He was on his way to the Dukeries to give his opinion on a Henri Manguin, a disputed Klee and to see a pair of Samuel Palmers nobody had heard of before. Victor Burden had been excited; he'd have a look, but he'd stay no longer than an hour.

He stayed less.

Arriving at five to ten, he'd shaken hands, been taken straight to the studio where he walked, apparently casually, round the hanging sketches. Occasionally he lifted a hand to a drawing, and waved it as if somehow to shift or distort the figures; he made no comment. When he had done the round once, he repeated it, stopping longer at one or two, though Worth could see no overriding pattern in his choice. 'Good,' he said, in the end. 'Good.' The foreign voice seemed misty, hoarse. 'You're acquiring energy. Good.' He laughed mischievously at the primed wood and its massive stand. 'It will be like moving a brick wall,' he said. His brown shoes, dark as a chestnut, shone; the small hands, slightly gesticulating, revealed square gold cufflinks; the light-grey suit was fit for a visit to a ducal house. 'Are you ready?' he asked.

'I shall have to be?' Worth grudged it. 'Shan't I?'

'When are you going to start?'

'Tomorrow.'

That surprised, for Walden lifted his head, and clashed his top teeth on the bottom set, quickly, ter, ter, ter, ter, ter. Worth had never heard another perform so. It transmogrified the place; this beautifully dressed elderly man, delicate-skinned, gnashing his teeth rhythmically.

'I wish you luck,' Walden said, dully enough. 'Do you want to paint this subject?'

'I'm getting myself near the position where I can't do any other.'

Walden perched in front of the white expanse, tiny hands tugging the points of his waistcoat.

'Yes. Good. Very good. It should be like a forest, in a high wind.' He waited for comment. 'A gale,' he said, as if words were the difficulty.

'At ground level, in the middle, there'll be places where it's still.' Why Worth bothered to argue he did not know; it seemed necessary.

'But you'd hear the riot up above; you know what happens in the top twigs.'

'I shall fill this mostly with people.'

Walden looked at the surface again to judge if the boast made sense.

'It's large,' he said. 'Large. Good.' He slapped the right-hand pillar of wood, turned gently away. 'Victor told you you're making a name in America. This exhibition's going to bring money.' He nodded. 'Paint hard before it happens.'

'Why do you say that?'

'So you'll acquire good, workman's, workingman's habits.

155

You're the fellow in the street. Except for your gifts, which are great. Cultivate them. Good?' He moved fast to tap a pencil sketch of Jo Feaver which was pinned to the baize of the noticeboard. 'I'll buy that from you.'

'Have it,' Worth said, pleased.

'No. Put her face in Jerusalem.'

He held out his hand, made straight for the door. In the corridor Worth said, 'I take it that Arab thing's off.'

'I've heard nothing. Nothing at all.'

He shook hands again, fingernails were pointed, and drove his large car away. The street seemed empty.

Next morning Worth rose at his usual time, crumbled through a breakfast similar to the one of the previous day, washed up, tidied the kitchen and changed the bedclothes as he did each Saturday. As he found his way past these chores, he kept glancing at his clock, accusing himself of wasting time, putting back the hour of starting. At five minutes to nine he stood in front of his whitened board.

He had decided against squaring the space; he'd draw free hand.

In the dark morning, he switched on his lights and began. The first hour, passing quickly, saw little done, except that he knew where the wild Christ would ride, and how large he and his motor-bike would be. That rough outline, he began with that; though it was sketched without detail it challenged him, seemed to call out the arabesques of faces, spring-green trees, red-brick houses, the clouds of March and April. He drew with hesitation at first, then with rapidity, and then with a stupefied pleasure, knowing that he could alter, erasing and reworking the light lines; and, as he laboured at the minutiae of pointing noses and fingers, the inclination of mortar in nearby houses, the tendency of distant streets or to-be-blue gaps in the clouds all directed themselves towards the central, interesting space where the black-leather, stud-spotted Son of Man would glower.

He took half an hour for lunch, stale cheese cobs and black coffee, and resumed with concentration. The throng pushing near the central figure all demonstrated ecstasies of fervour by

156

their posture, worship, yearning, adoration, flattery; while a few detested Him, showing repugnance, contempt, but nowhere indifference. Incredulity would stamp itself on some faces, but men rushed to tear off branches, slung down their jackets and football scarves and bonnets, the girls sang and waved and kicked, children ran shouting, dogs leapt. The smaller groups in the distance pursued their own vivid expressions of joy; one bunch let off a funnel of soaring balloons, a Salvation Army band marched puffing, tiny bricklayers slashed with their trowels and their labourers, hods piled, ascended (what other word?) the ladders to the second storeys of council houses in the New Jerusalem; a sober band knelt writing posters, a crocodile of marshalled children marched the wrong way and into the school foyer, a solitary prophet handed pamphlets to rushing enthusiasts who did not even bother to grab before dropping them; a man and woman had flung off their clothes and were dancing naked in an empty alley unobserved; the old cowered behind their windows; a rent collector, a windowcleaner and a mail van did their humdrum rounds.

It was past six when he finished; he did not cook for himself, but sat exhausted, gnawing at bread and jam. He walked the streets for an hour, soaked himself in the bath, was asleep by 9.30. Against his custom, he painted for six hours on Sunday, and on Tuesday grudged the time he spent on his newspaper work, not even trying and yet turning out a product adequate as usual.

After a week and six days, the picture stood off, shone out from its board, detailed and in turmoil, brighter, more garish, the figures livelier in thick colour, only slightly twisted towards caricature, humanity guyed into glory, thick or intelligent dancing themselves dizzy, God-possessed. He had grasped his nettle, like a child coming to first grips with the Protean slipperiness of language, but more quickly; the innocent eye instructed the cunning hand.

He ought to have looked like God on his work, but was jaded and decided he'd have to take a day off, eat, drink and be idle. On Friday night he rang Ursula, to ask for her company in Derbyshire.

157

'That would have been lovely,' she said, when he outlined his plan. 'But I can't.'

It dashed him; usually she complained that he left all arrangements to her and taunted that she'd put the flag out on the day he made his mind up for the pair of them.

'I kept meaning to ring you.' Her voice was subdued. 'I've heard nothing of you.'

He explained what he'd been at.

'That sounds good. I'm glad.'

He waited, could hear her breathing.

'It's like this,' she began, stopped. 'I've found someone else.'

'This Stout man?'

'Don't be ridiculous. That was nothing. You won't know him, but I'm living with him. It's only by chance you caught me in here when I came up to see my dad.'

'What's he say about it?'

'And what's that to do with anything?' She coughed. 'I'm sorry, John, but we didn't seem to be getting anywhere.'

'I've been busy.'

'I'm not blaming you. It wouldn't have come to anything. I mean, you'd have to admit that. You had your concerns. I'm sorry. I ought to have told you. I've been remiss.'

'And you're happy?'

'Yes. I can say that we are. Really happy.'

'What does he do?' he asked.

'He worked at County Hall. But he's taken A levels this summer and he's starting a law degree next week.'

'How old is he?'

'Twenty-two. He left school at sixteen; his parents wouldn't keep him on in the sixth form. Said they couldn't afford it. He's had to do it all for himself.'

'He's younger than you.'

'Three years. Nearly four. It's not a great deal. It means I shall be able to support him.'

'Another lame dog,' he said.

'That's not how I see it. I'm sorry, John, I ought to have told you before, but all this developed suddenly. It sounds foolish, but it wasn't.'

'I wish you all the best,' he said glumly.

'Thanks, John. I'm sorry. I really am. You're going to be somebody. Important. You don't need me.' Cold comfort spewed. 'You don't, not at all. I don't know if you need anybody.' She waited; he had nothing to say, and she rang off. Perhaps the vigour of his work in the past two weeks had knocked the energy out of him, but his hands trembled, he felt cold, sick. He could no more put a dab of paint on his picture than fly over the moon. Lacking will, he struggled up, rang Josephine Feaver.

A man answered, knowledgeably. No, he was sorry, but Jo wasn't there, she'd gone off last Thursday to Paris with Edwin Smith; they'd be back early next week, or at least that's what they had said. He thought it was some sort of celebration, but he wasn't sure, could be business, but he'd leave a message for her.

'Just tell her John Worth rang.'

That set the man off again. 'Chap who's just done her portrait? Very good, that. Very, very good.' The panegyrics crackled over the line, comfortless, and Worth thanked him bleakly.

He telephoned Millicent Turnbull.

'Tomorrow? Saturday?' she repeated. 'Well, I was going to do some more at the drawing room. I've started.'

'Take the day off.'

'You should ask Ursula.'

'It's all over between us.'

She did not comment, but they entered into negotiation, listless on his part, assertive on hers. She must have time to shop, and they'd travel in her car, he paying the petrol if he liked. She'd be at his front door at half-past ten. She'd leave the choice of hotels for lunch to him. At the end of this banal exchange, she said, 'Thank you, John. This is a godsend to me.'

She had never used his Christian name before.

Next morning, she arrived five minutes late, in a smart denim suit, and asked if they could drink a cup of coffee together, because she enjoyed anticipation. 'The trip will never be as

159

good as I think it will,' she said.

'You wait.' He felt waggish; the trouble with Ursula either left him untouched or had not yet registered its pain. They carted tall mugs into the studio, where he stood her in front of *The Entry*.

'What can I say?' Her mouth dropped open, her eyes were held wide. She gave a squeak or two, of pleasure, excitement, surprise. 'Don't you want to get on with it?'

'No.'

'It's striking. There's a lad in our office and he talks about whanging things about; he means throwing them hard. All these roads, and little people, and hedges seem to be whanging themselves at the man on the motor-bike. It's boiling over, isn't it? And so bright. Your paint's thick. It doesn't look dry.'

She stroked her pale chin, sipped her coffee, glancing at the picture as if it would bite.

He watched her; she could not say much, but burst out, in the end, breathily. 'It's physical, isn't it? I don't know much about this sort. . . '

Months later, in London, when the press had taken the painting up, when clergymen were theologizing and clawing each other's eyes out in the correspondence columns of *The Times* over it, when one distinguished critic had complained about its lack of intellectual or emotional content and had been savaged by an even more distinguished colleague, when Worth had been interviewed a dozen times on television, when one could not open the posh Sundays without seeing the thing or a detail from it or letters about it, when three American agents were bidding against each other for it, the painter remembered this pale girl, with her denim skirt, her navy tights, standing there lipping the rim of her mug. He drew her, later, but never achieved the heavenly innocence. Physical, isn't it? It was.

Now, as he watched her she seemed to struggle with herself, her loss of home and husband, to stutter something out to reward his gigantic effort. Later, when the bouquets and few, very few, brickbats were flying, he'd remember it as *An Angel Judges an Earthly Masterpiece*, the silence of heaven in face of puny man, and that twisted the whole, so that his sketch was fatuous.

'Can you see it?' he asked. 'You're not wearing your glasses.'

'I've got my new contact lenses on.'

They paused.

'It's marvellous,' she said. 'Superb. Do other people like it?'

'You're the first.'

She blushed, violently; the colour change shouted.

'I've started the room,' she said. 'I've really cleaned it up, and I've got one coat of emulsion on the walls.'

'Well done.'

They walked back to the warmth of the kitchen.

The day out was quietly memorable, though he felt clumsy, as if he were easing himself at her expense, or might knock her over with some crudity of remark or gesture. They lunched at the Peacock in Beardsley, finally at home among the glassware and pile carpets, sitting by a radiator under a window with stained-glass scrolls fit for a Victorian chapel. Millicent tackled a huge steak Diane, elbows working, enjoying mouthfuls as the sky brightened. She drank one glass of red wine, chose Black Forest gâteau, dowsed it with thick cream, and smiled.

'You'll be ruined,' she said. He would remember that when a year later he had to employ an accountant to control the cataract of cheques.

As they walked from the dining room, they met Edwin Smith and Jo Feaver, who had been eating at the far end, out of their sight.

'Well, well, well,' said Smith, after introductions. 'Come and have a drink.'

'I thought you were in Paris.'

'Paris or Beardsley, we can't tell the difference.'

They sat in a corner, in a day-deprived, crowded, bright lounge. Millicent drank bitter lemon but Worth, already dizzy, picked whisky.

'He's painting a marvellous picture,' Millicent let out, five minutes later.

'Only one?' Smith, facetiously.

She looked at him, her face quite serious, her lips trembling

161

as if she'd launch a violence of invective at him. It was a sight. The wren, 'the most diminutive of birds', guarded her chick. Smith coughed, momentarily abashed.

Worth gave a gruff account of work in progress.

'Still nothing, though,' Jo asked, 'about that Arab thing?'

Why did that loom so important when a year later it meant next to nothing?

They talked about art, or Smith and Jo did; Worth sat mindlessly, seeing the world as the world's not, in the euphoria of a student's Saturday night out. Millicent perched on the edge of her cushion, erect, not willing to lose a word. She hardly spoke, looked no more than sixteen so that her wedding ring seemed pretentious, her widowhood unmentionable.

'What are you doing this afternoon?' Smith.

'Walking.' Worth.

'I'd offer to go with you, but I'd slow the party down.' Smith laughed, beerily, though he drank cognac. 'Tell you what. We'll have tea in our room here. At five-thirty? The best of the day will be over then.'

'I couldn't eat a thing,' Millicent said.

'Go and work an appetite up. Toast, and an urn of tea, and their rich cherry cake.'

Worth and Millicent walked but were disappointed even when the weather kept fine. They had not brought a map, and therefore dared not wander far from the lay-by where they had parked their car; the afternoon's exercise consisted of three different, equally uninteresting loops, along hedged lanes, back to their base.

'We should have gone further and higher,' he said, 'and then we could have seen where we were and what we were up to.'

To walk with her itself had drawbacks. For a start, she stationed herself on his left, a yard, or a yard and a half, behind him, and held the position. She kept up without difficulty, even when he deliberately quickened the pace, but made no attempt to push ahead, or check progress by drawing attention to matters of interest. She inaugurated no conversation, though she answered cheerfully, even lengthily, any observation he made. There was no need for physical contact in that she was

162

clearly fit, used to walking, so that it seemed unnecessary to put out a hand to help her up rough gradients or over puddled ruts. They walked. The tip of her nose turned pink; she needed to blow it often, with a man's handkerchief.

They took exercise, in not inclement weather in not unpleasant country, and that was the length and breadth of it. The effect of the wine, the spirits, had evaporated; at least he was not painting and the air struck fresh, as he put one foot after the other, but he felt he should demand more. God knew what. A jilted man kept company with a widow woman. A passing labourer gave them good day, seeing what? Lovers? Young father and daughter? Did God know that, either?

At the top of a hill, where they had as near a prospect as they'd find today, though that was screened by the still leafy trees and hedges, he stopped suddenly, turned. She halted as quickly, without surprise.

'Are you enjoying yourself?' he asked.

'Oh, yes.'

'It's a bit raw, isn't it?'

'I'm warm. And I think I shall be able to eat some of Mr Smith's toast.'

'It's only just half-four. Are you enjoying this?'

'Yes. I would never have come out on my own, and yet now, I'm not likely to forget this afternoon.'

'The country's dull.'

'Do you think so? I thought – ' she looked about her, downwards, and then moved to pick up nine inches of bare twig from the path – 'you'd see this as a marvellous object to paint. Hold eternity in the palm of your hand.' He could not tell whether she was mocking him, but thought not.

'Did you go out much with Teddy?'

'When we first . . . Before we were married.'

'To Derbyshire?'

'Sometimes. He didn't take as much exercise as he should have recently. I thought we should have a dog, but I'm glad now we didn't.'

'Wouldn't it be company?'

'Yes, but the wrong sort. It would make a fuss of me, and I of

163

it, but it wouldn't be what I wanted. With Ted, well, we hadn't been married long enough to get domesticated. We hadn't dropped into ruts. Not when we were both at work. We quarrelled, sometimes.' Her voice touched a higher, hesitant register. 'Not seriously. He could be an old stick-in-the-mud. And a grumbler. And he was touchy beyond reason about things like punctuality.'

'I remember.'

'We used to talk about you. He didn't know anybody quite like you and that left him a bit suspicious and envious. I used to say that I thought you were lonely, and he'd laugh and tell me you made capital out of it. "If the milkman forgets to leave the milk," he said, "all I can do is swear, and take it out of the kids. But Worthy" – he called you that, did you know? – "gets his own back out of his paintbox, and everybody profits. He lives on his own, and works on his own, and that's the beauty of it." I used to ask him, "What about Ursula?" but all he answered was, "She's just a pair of knickers to take down." He could be crude. I don't think he ever made you out, but somehow he was delighted you could earn a living. He wanted a world where people read books, and looked at pictures, and listened to music, and enjoyed science for what it demanded not what it gave, and it pleased him that he knew somebody who, who, well, contributed to such a place.'

Worth put his teeth together, pulled off a mitten and held a hand out to her. She took it briefly, impersonally in her gloved right, and let it go as she stared out to a rough grass slope, neutral tussocks, a small jungle of brambles, a tractor track.

'Thanks,' he said.

'He talked like this to me.'

What she had said had an air of quotation, but he guessed it more likely to be from one of her husband's WEA homilies than from a fireside confession. Again, one didn't know, could not know.

'Shall we walk a bit further?' he asked.

The summit was flat, a hedged plateau, but the lane suddenly swerved at right angles without losing height. They took the turn, but the lane preserved its monotony of hedges, small trees, rutted surface.

'This should start to go downhill.'

'Everything got on his nerves towards the end.' She had caught up and continued a conversation that had been going on, he guessed, in her head. 'He thought Elspeth had tried to squeeze too much out of him, and Natalie's broken marriage bothered him because he could do nothing about it. He liked to think there was action he could take. And Piers was so casual about what he was doing. To Ted, becoming a doctor of philosophy of Oxford University was like being made a saint, but Piers was in no hurry, and spoke as if it didn't matter or he didn't care and the examiners were mental cases who'd pass you one day and fail you the next on exactly the same grounds. And then the school, but you know all about that.' He did not take his eyes off her as she talked, but she delivered somewhere over his shoulder towards a hawthorn bush. 'There was me. I must have been as much a worry.'

'No,' Worth said.

'He married Elspeth. He should have stuck by her. That's what he thought. They must have been happy in their early years. From things he sometimes let out about holidays and the children. They went to Italy in their first car. Elspeth changed. She wanted to get on. She had been a kind of second, now she was going to be first.'

'You didn't mind? Being second?'

'I was in trouble. The course was getting me down. And this Jeremy business. He picked me up, Teddy, he really did. I went to one of his classes, just by chance, just because somebody I knew attended, so I tagged along. And we all had a half-pint afterwards. I talked to him first on one of his Saturday trips; we looked at earliest evidences of the Industrial Revolution. I talked to him. And he invited me to his home. Elspeth was nice, what bit I saw of her. And then once he put his arms round me because I was crying, and he kissed me. It surprised me. He said right out that he loved me. When I think of it now, I can hardly believe it, because he was usually so cagey, and careful, and nervous before he did anything. But it happened. Exactly like that. You don't believe me, I know, but it did.'

He shifted his feet; this was too like eavesdropping.

'That's what finished him,' she continued. 'He expected to be punished. It was built into his personality. He shouldn't have taken up with me; he shouldn't have deserted Elspeth. He had to pay for it.'

'It must have been hard for you.'

'Occasionally. I didn't notice. We had such good times. We were getting it together. That's how it seemed. I don't know whether what I'm telling you is right; it's how I see it now, after his breakdown and his death. Thank God I'm not pregnant.'

'Did you . . . ?'

'No. I was on the pill. I was when I first met him, because of Jeremy. But Ted didn't want children. We never even considered it. But there are mistakes.'

'Might you have had them, later?'

'How can I tell? Ted thought our marriage would break up. He kept saying so. Lately. I couldn't understand that at the time. But it must have been his guilt.'

'And you?'

'I didn't know what I was doing. At first. I was incapable of making decisions. But going about with him, meeting secretly, and all that, was better by a million miles than what I had. He saved me. I was going down, fast. I'm not the suicidal type, but I'd have slit my wrists, I tell you.'

The declaration made, she relaxed, turned her fingers to touching her clothes. The little face was peaky, the nose redder, but she was ready to walk on.

He remembered this a year later, in the flush of his success, when he was getting ready for a promotional trip to America and Edgar Quinn rang up to say Ursula had split with her young man and had come back home.

'Will you see her?' Quinn asked, whining as usual, but certain what he wanted.

'Yes.' He started to explain how much of his time was occupied.

'She won't ask you. I said, "Give John a tinkle," but not her. Not now your photo's always in the papers.'

'Has it upset her?'

'You know our Urse. Missus Bleddy know-all herself. But

her face is set like a rock, and she snaps my head off every time I open my mouth, or ignores me as if she's deaf. Ah, it has. But she'd sooner cut her tongue out than tell me. And she's got no friends, no more nor I have.'

She'd visited him, in her smartest clothes, and glanced at his work in progress, heard about his meetings with the famous, had held herself like steel so that when he put his arms round her she'd pushed him off, her beautiful face ugly as a lump of putty.

'Will you come out to lunch on Saturday?' he had asked. He left for New York on Monday.

'I've a meeting. I can't.' He didn't believe it.

'Sunday, then?'

'I must cook my dad's dinner. He's neglected himself.'

Worth had tried. Now he gave up, but held out his hand to her. She took it, with her gloves on, looked ready to kick his shins, and turned her back on his triumph and his television interviews and his money, hating herself.

'Shall we walk on?' he asked Millicent. 'We mustn't be late.'

She smiled, still half immersed in her confession, but released, absolved by it. Just as they began to walk a gust of wind from nowhere, for all Worth could remember it had been flat calm the moment before, dipped to hit the hillside, the hedges, hacked through the branches of the trees, knocking down a comical shower of leaves, apparently green still, good for weeks. The noise burst, rustling the thick lace of twigs, rasping leaves and bending the ends of strong branches. Birds flew up, buffeted, scattered and dropped. The rush of wind was so like the blast of an explosion that Worth half expected to hear the boom; that was impossible, he decided, but he held himself ready, vainly. The squall died off; the hedgerows were silent, surviving leaves hung limp, but small new heaps of broken foliage littered the path.

'That was something,' Millicent said.

'What, though?'

'Like a little whirlwind.'

They waited for the next; it did not come; the late afternoon renewed its autumnal monotony.

'That was a phenomenon,' she said.

167

'The wind bloweth where it listeth.'

The quotation satisfied them so that they affected a jaunty march back to the car. Worth tried later to paint the *coup de vent*, but failed to please himself. The pictures were praised, sold immediately, but they seemed over-dramatic, stagey, histrionic, with leaves streaming straight, or masses of colour whipped from one shade to the violent, ruffled next. He could not stop the blast; he had caught the inordinate vigour of the squall but not its ephemeral essence. The mind-stopping power of this fling consisted in the sudden nature of its demise. Twigs and leaves had rattled, whistled, scoured each other, and had frozen suddenly still. A thousand noises had become one silence. Static paint depicting junketing movement could not depict this. An oddity.

They reached the Peacock exactly at 5.30.

'My shoes aren't very clean,' Millicent said, doubtfully. Josephine waited in the foyer, led them immediately upstairs.

Smith's room was large, and bedless. The bathroom matched it. A table was laid with a starched cloth, china, silver. A uniformed man and a boy arrived with trolley, tea, toast, cheese, jam, relish, four sorts of cake.

'Shall I draw the curtains, sir?' the man inquired.

'No thanks.'

'That's right. You hold on to the last of the daylight.' The servants withdrew.

Josephine poured the tea; the visitors enjoyed themselves; Smith toying with toast asked Millicent about the new picture. In the beautiful warmth of the room, with the grey shapes of cloud like ill-drawn continents on the faded cold sea-green of the sky, Worth knew peace. Sometimes, rarely, his father or mother had taken him as a child into a teashop, for an iced bun, and then he had become part of an opulent life, fat men licking butter from their fingers, thin ladies cutting up their cream fancies with small knives, and he had been proud, and safe, and in another world.

In answer to Millicent, Josephine explained that Smith had been able to book the room because he was a shareholder in the brewery which owned the place. Worth thought he disliked

168

privilege. Millicent grew garrulous about *The Entry*, though the painter said next to nothing, and Smith was charmed, humming deeply, as he listened.

'Miss here,' he told Worth in the end, 'has really pushed on with that monograph. And it's not just scissors and paste, either. She's getting ideas.'

'About John?' The excited Milly.

'Of course. She's clever.'

'How do you know that?'

'She's convinced me, that's why.'

'Then tell us what she's said.'

'She can do that for herself. In any case, she ought to try them out on the man now she's got him here, to see what he thinks.'

'Why?' Millicent exceeded expectation, was outside herself, outsize. 'They will only be opinions, anyway. And John may not know why he paints as he does.'

'He may not want to know,' Jo said.

They all looked at Worth, who defended his face with a teacup.

'I'm an academic painter,' he said, gruffly.

'That's right.' Jo agreed too quickly to please. 'You had this marvellously strict training, and it suited you. But you're beginning to grow out of it.'

'I hope not.'

'Wrong words, then. To grow past it. To utilize it differently.' He didn't answer that.

'Go on,' Smith encouraged. 'Tell him why.'

'You've lived on your own.'

She spoke the words simply, but with confidence, as if they were a releasing spell or the key to a code. The other three looked about them, until Worth made a small, comic gesture of incomprehension.

'You've lived on your own from choice,' she continued. 'Because that's what you wanted. And I don't think . . .' She leaned back, like a boxer keeping his guard up. 'You're not going to like this much: I don't think that basically you're concerned with human beings.'

'That "basically" is put in to soften the blow,' Smith instructed Millicent. 'Doesn't mean much.'

169

'You live on your own,' she said again. 'You keep yourself to yourself.'

'How do you make that out?' Worth, wounded.

'From looking at those execution pictures, and the sketches for *Christ's Entry*. It's not the people, it's the patterns. And that's why they're so good. You look on humanity in a different, new, striking way. It's not a man shot, it's a shot man's body.'

'That's beyond me,' he snapped.

'I can see I've annoyed you. But it's right. And it's your strength. I'm not saying you're inhuman, and don't fall in love, or feel grief or disappointment or anger like the rest of us. You do. But by keeping yourself apart you've strengthened the painter, the image-maker.'

'Very fine,' Worth said.

'Isn't it a great drawback for an artist not to be interested in human beings?' Millicent.

'What do you say to that, Worth?' Smith, delighted.

'It is.'

'I didn't say you weren't interested,' Jo objected. She spoke like a schoolma'am admonishing a disobedient crocodile of charges. 'I claimed the opposite. But because he –' the pronoun emphasized her authority – 'chooses to live on his own, not to engage himself too intimately, then it has stressed the technical. . .'

'Doesn't one underline the other?' Smith. 'The first maintain the second?'

'Oh, yes, yes.' She spoke impatiently. 'And it's next door to impossible to disentangle them. When both are fully locked, and both are enormously strong or deep, the result is Rembrandt. That doesn't happen too often.'

'What do you think, Mrs Turnbull?'

'About John?'

'Yes.' The politest of wide, ironical smiles.

'It's right. Not that John isn't human. I mean, why should he take me out this afternoon? But he keeps himself at a distance. He protects himself.'

'But that is a drawback?'

'Yes. No. Now I come to think about it.' Her cheeks were

flushed with the comfort of the room or the heat of the argument. 'One can become too immersed, and that stops . . . My husband was rather like . . . No, that's not true, either. Is John a great painter?' She flung the question in Jo's face, suddenly, as though it had been generated whole in her puzzlement.

'One of the most interesting? Yes. Limited? Yes.'

'Not Rembrandt?'

'There's only been one.'

'Will he improve, widen his scope?' Smith, the question-monger. 'And how?'

'I look forward to his painting of the sea.'

That happened when the money began to flash; he spent three summer months in Cornwall, and a cold January–February in Suffolk, fighting his way into the light, and out again on to the paper.

Worth did not care now; dashed but uncertain, he felt the discussion did not concern him, did not matter to him.

'I am decorating a room,' Millicent announced. Her statement dropped laughable. 'And in a way it's connected with John's painting for the Arabian prince. That sounds daft, but it is.'

Smith made encouraging noises.

'If he got the commission, I was going to start. Teddy didn't encourage me. He wanted it left dirty, like a part of his past. But now, I've started. And I shall finish it in a few weeks. But John won't . . .'

'So they're not connected.' Jo, brightly.

'My husband has died.'

The path of the argument, illogical, emotionally rough, did not elude. It told on them.

'Don't worry,' Smith said. 'I won't see him on the breadline. He can do a few quick jobs with acrylic in my supermarkets. I won't see him starve.'

After John's exhibition, and success, the Arab mural spouted fine gold. Walden convinced the client he had left the negotiation too long, that he could have had a Worth master-piece for the price of a carpet, but now, now . . . Hours were in short supply; money needed to shout. By the time Worth had

171

found and conceded three weeks, they were begging him to return to the bucolic, a pond with winter trees in Burwell Park, and his accountant had complained it was hardly worth his bother. 'Get him to smuggle diamonds in, and pay you with them.'

Millicent's drawing room had by then been long completed, and while he was dabbing in St John's Wood she smartly married a young accountant at St John's, Carrington. She and her new husband kept the old house. Much of Turnbull's rubbish provided potash for the garden; Piers and Natalie were welcome, but never called, and the place shone spick and span, woodwork light, polyurethane glistening, the former darkness dispersed, the brown paint, the old love stripped off.

Worth remembered this day when almost two years later he sold his parents' house, drew his last cartoon, and moved, against his oath, to London. He could have kept the old bricks and mortar, he was rich enough, as a symbol, but he refused to be sentimental. It did him no harm to be exiled; this place with its Bulwell stone walls, its lime trees, slate roofs had become a Beulah land, a marriage place, towards which the bachelor bothered by his women looked back and forward.

Now they ate toast, and Worth licked his fingers.

'Tell you what,' Smith said. 'We'll drive off and see this masterpiece.'

'It's not finished.'

'No picture's finished. That's one thing I've learned from Jo.'

'And you'll come back here tonight?' Millicent asked.

'Surely. We're on holiday. But we shan't rest until we've seen it. Half an hour looking, and a cup of coffee. We don't miss chances. We'll finish here, and give you a few minutes' start to get the boiler on.'

Their laughter lit the room. As Worth and Millicent left, Josephine was drawing the curtains and thinking out loud what she'd wear for the excursion. When the two drew up outside Worth's house, Smith's car was already there waiting for opening time.

On the pavement, in evening dews and damps, they laughed together again.

172